P

IN A CLA

SC

From first-day-of-term nerves to falling in love with the teacher, from a reluctant footballer to a cricket match on the school bus, these wonderfully varied stories reveal things about school you've never dreamed of!

Twelve talented and well-known writers, from Jan Mark and Gene Kemp to Tim Kennemore and George Layton, cover the whole spectrum of school life, which can be terrifying, exciting, hilarious or just plain horrible!

Barbara Ireson grew up on the south coast of England, but now lives in France with her husband. She retired from teaching to concentrate on her writing and has written and edited numerous books.

IN A CLASS OF THEIR OWN

School Stories

Selected by
Barbara Ireson

PUFFIN BOOKS IN ASSOCIATION
WITH FABER AND FABER

Puffin Books, Penguin Books Ltd, Harmondsworth, Middlesex, England
Viking Penguin Inc., 40 West 23rd Street, New York, New York 10010, U.S.A.
Penguin Books Australia Ltd, Ringwood, Victoria, Australia
Penguin Books Canada Ltd, 2801 John Street, Markham, Ontario, Canada L3R 1B4
Penguin Books (N.Z.) Ltd, 182–190 Wairau Road, Auckland 10, New Zealand

First published by Faber and Faber 1985
Published in Puffin Books 1987

Made and printed in Great Britain by
Richard Clay Ltd, Bungay, Suffolk

Contents

◇◇

Acknowledgements

The editor is grateful for permission to use the following copyright material: "A Knife with Sixteen Blades", reprinted by permission of Faber and Faber Ltd from *Autumn Term* by Antonia Forest.

"The Trouble with Donovan Croft", an extract reprinted from *The Trouble with Donovan Croft* by Bernard Ashley (1974) by permission of Oxford University Press. © Bernard Ashley 1974.

"Seymour's Century" by Jan Mark, reprinted by permission of the author and Murray Pollinger.

"The Scar" by Margaret Biggs, reprinted by permission of the author.

"The Disappearing Abolisher" from *Professor Branestawm's Treasure Hunt* by Norman Hunter is reproduced by permission of The Bodley Head.

A Knife with Sixteen Blades

<><><><><><><><><><><><><><><><><><><><><><><><><><><><><><><><>

Antonia Forest

Train journeys, Nicola decided, were awfully dull. After the first half-hour no one seemed to want to talk any more, so that unless you had something to read you sat and looked at Karen and Lawrie and Rowan opposite or right and left at Ann and Ginty. Actually, Nicola had a book on her lap (Karen had seen to that before they left Victoria) but she wasn't in the mood for reading. She seldom was. Nicola's world had to be very calm and settled before she could sit down quietly with a book, a remedy frequently suggested by her weary relations as an antidote to Nicola's general air of being all agog.

It had been suggested very often in the last week or so; for even the excitement of going into town almost daily with her mother and Lawrie to be measured for their new uniforms and buy the startling number of new under-

11

clothes necessary for school, and (crowning glory) eat
lunch and tea in a restaurant and order exactly what
they liked (which meant that Lawrie stuck to chicken
and ice-cream and Nicola dodged all over the menu to
make sure she was missing nothing), had not, as Rowan
so hopefully prophesied, tired her out. She still came
back and stood on one leg near Karen or Rowan or Ann
(Ginty was too unreliable) and went on asking questions:

"Will Miss Keith see us when we get there? Where do
we go first? Do new girls have to sing on First Night like
they do in books? Who will be games captain this term?
Mother says I can wear Ginty's old blazer. Can I? Do
people? Wouldn't it be better if Lawrie wore her hair a
different way so that we don't look so much like twins?
Will people be funny about it? Shall we share a sisters'
room with the rest of you?"

"I hope not," said Rowan emphatically. "The first thing
I do when I get back is look at the dormitory lists; and if
we are in the same I'm going straight to Matron to
protest."

"Oh, Rowan. Why?"

"Because I like my nights quiet, peaceful and undis-
turbed. I can't honestly feel that they'd be that with you
around. And do go away, Nick. I'm supposed to have read
this wretched book by the time I get back."

Nicola went away and found Giles, who was the eldest,
and was doing nothing at all but lie peacefully on his
back in the sun.

"They won't tell me things," she complained, sitting
down cross-legged beside him. "And I want to know so as
to be prepared."

"Prepared for what?" asked Giles sleepily.

"Just prepared. So that I don't do anything awfully
silly and have people laughing at me like they do. And so
that I know what it's going to be like."

"No good worrying about being laughed at. There are
sure to be thousands of new brats all making the same

12

mistakes at the same time. And as for telling you what it's like—no one can do that."

"Why not?"

"Because, my idiot sister, the same thing looks quite different to different people. Karen can't possibly tell you what the kindergarten—"

"IIIA," said Nicola indignantly.

"Kindergarten," said Giles firmly, "looks like from the Sixth. Father tried to tell me what the Navy was like before I got there, but it wasn't like that at all. Not to me, anyway."

"Oh," said Nicola.

So she had, to the relief of her family, almost stopped asking questions. Not entirely, of course. But they only came out now when she had to ask or burst.

The train journey continued dull. Nicola swung her legs and looked crossly round the carriage, piecing together from her own and her sisters' uniforms the things she knew about Kingscote. The three black felt hats in the rack with the blue and scarlet hat-bands meant that Rowan and Ann and Ginty were seniors. The fourth hat, with the plain scarlet band, was Karen's and meant she was a prefect. Head girl actually, thought Nicola accurately, and she has a special badge to pin her tie. The two scarlet berets with the bright blue crest belonged to Nicola and Lawrie and showed they were juniors. What else was there? There was Rowan's plain blue tie because she was in the netball team, and Ginty's striped girdle for second eleven hockey. Ann wore a Guide badge on her coat—but that wasn't particularly a school thing. Nicola yawned and kicked Ginty accidentally-on-purpose.

"Couldn't Lawrie and I go and stand in the corridor for a bit?" suggested Nicola hopefully, when the commotion had died down a little.

"For heaven's sake, let them," said Rowan. "If Nick's starting to fidget no one'll have any peace."

"Well—all right," said Karen. "But *don't* go and fall

13

out of a window. Miss Keith wouldn't be a bit pleased if
the train were late because one of the school was careless
about a little thing like that."

She spoke in her girl's voice which had returned to her a
day or two before term began, making Giles salute and say:
"Yes, *ma'am*" in a way Karen found particularly aggravat-
ing. But Nicola was only concerned with what Karen said,
not how she said it. She sprang to her feet, knocking Ann's
book from her hand, trod on Rowan's foot and tumbled out
into the corridor followed by Lawrie. Rowan closed the
carriage door firmly behind them.

"Good," said Nicola. "Now we can talk."

Lawrie nodded. Like Nicola she was thin and blue-eyed
with straight sun-bleached hair and an expression of
alert enquiry. But she talked less than Nicola, and
although she was just as interested, she was inclined to
leave it to Nicola to find out and tell her all about it when
she had done so.

"What time is it?" asked Nicola.

Lawrie looked at her watch, a parting present from her
parents. Nicola could have had a watch too, but when she
had been told to choose her present she had plumped for
the knife with sixteen blades which had dazzled her for
months every time she passed the ironmonger's window
where it was the centre-piece. Her father had warned her
that if she had the knife she would have to do without a
watch till she was twenty-one. Nicola thought this no
drawback. There were always clocks. And bells. Especially
in school. One wouldn't need a watch. Whereas a knife
with sixteen blades—she took it out of her pocket and
stroked it affectionately.

"It's ten to three," said Lawrie.

"Another hour," said Nicola despairingly. "I do think
trains are dull, even in the corridor."

"I wonder if we'll like it," said Lawrie nervously. She
meant, as Nicola promptly realized, since Lawrie had
been saying the same thing every night for weeks, school,
not the train.

14

"I don't see why not. The others do."

"They're used to it," said Lawrie.

"So will we be used to it," said Nicola firmly. "In two weeks, Giles said."

"I hope Giles knows," said Lawrie. She sighed deeply.

A few compartments down, a door slid back and a girl came out. Like Lawrie and Nicola she wore the scarlet beret of the juniors. She looked at them and then pretended not to look, leaning against the partition and staring at the scenery.

Nicola nudged Lawrie. "Is she new too, d'you think?"

"I don't know," whispered Lawrie.

"I think she may be or she'd be inside talking to people," decided Nicola. She edged down the corridor and said:

"Are you new like us?"

The other girl turned and grinned. She had short, rough dark hair, and her face was tanned the colour of a brown egg. Her eyes were a lighter brown, with greenish flecks in them. Nicola, whose favourite looks just then were sleek black hair and grey eyes, could not decide whether she thought her pretty or not. Lawrie, who had already decided, thought she wasn't.

"New as paint," said the other girl.

"Good," said Nicola. "How old are you?"

"Twelve and a half; how old are you?"

"We're twelve. That's Lawrence and I'm Nicola. Nicola Marlow."

"Well," said the other girl, "I'm glad other people have odd names too. It makes me feel better." She had a dry, amused voice.

"They're not odd at all," said Nicola, affronted.

"Not odd," conceded the other girl, "but not ordinary. Not like Joan and Peggy and Betty."

"Well—no," admitted Nicola, "I suppose not."

"Now mine is definitely odd," said the other girl. "And you may as well know it at once and that will be two less people to tell. It's Thalia. Thalia Keith."

"Failure?" said Lawrie startled. She was further away than Nicola and the train had blurred the sound of Thalia's voice. "Why did they call you that? Because you weren't a boy? That's why they called me Lawrence, 'cos they'd got it all saved up."

"Not Failure." She said it patiently as though she had said it many times before. *"Thalia.* It's the name of the Comic Muse. Mother would have it, though Father did his best."

"It's quite all right," said Nicola politely. Privately, she thought it very odd indeed.

"It's terrible," said Thalia calmly. "But people call me Tim. And if you don't mind, I'd rather you began at once."

"All right. They call us Nick and Lawrie, actually. At least, they do at home."

"Tim, Nick and Lawrie," said Thalia thoughtfully. "Tom, Dick and Harry. No, I think our way's better. Did you say your name was Marlow?"

"Yes."

"Head girl's family?"

"How did you know?" asked Nicola, surprised. "Or have you got sisters here too?"

"Not sisters," said Tim impressively. "An aunt."

"An aunt?" said Nicola, horrified. "What kind of aunt?"

"The ordinary kind," said Tim. "Or perhaps not so ordinary. Actually it's—well, I call her Aunt Edith. You call her the Head."

"The headmistress?" said Lawrie unbelievingly. "Good gracious. She can't be."

"She is, though."

"How awful for you," said Nicola, deeply sympathetic. "It's bad enough being the head girl's sister. At least, I think it may be. But think of being related to Miss Keith."

"I don't. Not more often than I can help," said Tim. "I told Father that it was simply silly and that I'd much better go to another school—if I must go to school—"

16

"Haven't you been to school before?" Lawrie interrupted.

"Not properly. At least, not for long at a time. We were always shifting because Father wanted something new to paint. I've been to school in America and Spain and France and Italy and Holland—all over the place. So, of course, I don't know a thing except languages. I do know those."

"Gosh," said Nicola, uncertain whether she was impressed or merely astonished. "We haven't been to school either, much. Every time we started we always caught something. But we haven't caught anything now for six months—"

"Touch wood," said Lawrie hurriedly.

"Touch wood," agreed Nicola. "So Father said we'd better get to Kingscote while the going was good."

"It was Aunt Edith got at Father about me," said Tim gloomily. "He decided to come home for a bit and paint here, and of course Aunt Edith was asked to stay. And then she began finding out, in a nasty sort of way, all the things I didn't know—What were the Wars of the Roses, Thalia dear?—Don't know, Aunt Edith, and care less— you know the kind of thing—and then she sat down and had a long talk with Father and said the dear child simply must start her education, which hiking round Europe and America was *not*. And *I* said (when they mentioned it to me, which was pretty late in the day), If I must go to school I must, but not to Aunt Edith's seminary. And Aunt Edith said, Why? And I said, Because it's bound to be awkward. And Aunt Edith said, Nonsense, Thalia dear, of course you will be treated exactly like the others. And I said, That's just the point. If I go to an ordinary school—all right. But if I go to my aunt's school, I don't see why I *can't* be treated like the headmistress's niece. *Why* can't I have special privileges and sit in your garden and that kind of thing? She didn't see it, though," said Tim bitterly, "but I still don't see why not."

17

Nicola and Lawrence listened, fascinated. It had been impressed on them also, by both Karen and Rowan, that they were on no account to give themselves airs simply because they happened to be the head girl's sisters. They had accepted this dictum meekly, protesting: "Of course, not, Kay. We wouldn't dream of it." But there did seem to be something in what Tim said, although Nicola, at least, was aware that if she tried anything like that, Karen would certainly snub her, hard.

"Aunt Edith—I suppose I shall have to remember to call her Miss Keith—" continued Tim, "she was full of helpful hints about lying low and showing the other girls that there was no difference between us. But lying low sounds so *dull*. I don't see why I should have to pretend to be a nonentity just because I'm her niece, and she doesn't want to be accused of—of nepotism—"

"What's that?" asked Lawrie, horrified. "It sounds dreadful."

"It only means favouring your nephews. Or nieces too, I suppose. But I don't see why I should be expected to come to Kingscote and be quiet and dreary and—and *crushed*, when I could go somewhere else and be perfectly ordinary. I told Aunt Edith all that, and she laughed in that idiotic way grown-ups have, and said:'Never mind, Thalia. You'll soon settle down in the Third Remove and find your own level—' "

"Third Remove?" cried Lawrie. "Oh. What a pity!"

"Why?" asked Tim.

"Well, because we'll be in IIIA and I don't suppose we'll see much of you once we're there—"

"Do you know your form?" asked Tim, surprised. "I thought no one did until they'd taken the form exam. Aunt Edith said I'd be in the Third Remove because of only knowing languages. But I didn't know anyone else was told."

Nicola had gone rather red. She frowned at Lawrie.

"We don't know, really," she said awkwardly. "But all our family always have started in an A form and—well—

you know—we've got to, too."

"None of the others have ever been in a B form," supplemented Lawrie. "Not even Ginty and no one thinks she's a bit clever. And IIIA is the one for our age."

"Aunt Edith talked quite a lot about your family," said Tim, digging her hands into the pockets of her coat. "Karen, of course—she's the head girl, isn't she?— she thinks an awful lot of her. And what's the next one—Rowena—?"

"No. Rowan."

"Yes, of course. Sorry. Rowan. She's the one who's good at games, isn't she? She said—what was it?—something about her being an excellent person to have in a team because she always played best on a losing side."

Nicola and Lawrie blushed with pleasure. "Except for Giles, Rowan *is* the nicest," said Nicola. "Kay's all right, but she can be pretty snooty when she likes."

"And then there's—Ann, is it?—the Guide one, any-way. Aunt Edith said she was kind and competent—very good with juniors—and the other one—Virginia, I think she called her—"

"She is Virginia, really," said Lawrie, "But she's always called Ginty."

"Oh. Well, she said she was rather wild but that she had a lot of good stuff in her."

"She didn't say that on her report," commented Nicola. "She put, 'Virginia's conduct leaves much to be desired and she must make a real effort to improve'."

"There you are," said Tim impishly. "It just shows what hypocrites headmistresses really are."

"It does, doesn't it?" agreed Lawrie, deeply moved.

There was a silence for a moment. Then Nicola sighed. "It's an awful lot to live up to," she said sadly.

"How d'you mean?" asked Tim.

"Well, you can see for yourself the kind of reputations they've got. Kay's awfully clever, and Rowan can play anything, and Ann's a Patrol Leader and she's got her First Class, and Ginty—well, even Ginty's pretty good at games and people like her a lot—"

"And have you got to do all that too?"

"We must," said Lawrie earnestly. "We've simply got to be credits to the family. Specially as we're starting so late. All the others came to Kingscote when they were *nine*. We decided in the holidays," said Lawrie confidentially, ignoring Nicola's warning frown, "that first we've got to get into the junior netball team, so that next year Nick can be captain and me vice. And then—we've been Brownies at home, you know—so we're going to pass our Tenderfoot and fly up and get our Second Class badges all in one term."

"Do shut up, Lawrie," said Nicola gruffly, interrupting her at last. "It sounds so mad when you say it like that. It probably doesn't matter with Tim, but you can't go round *saying* things like that to people."

"'Vaulting ambition,'" said Tim solemnly, shaking her head at Lawrie, "'which o'er leaps itself, and falls on the other.'"

"Gosh," said Lawrie abashed. "Whatever's that?"

"That's Macbeth," said Tim, "and look what happened to him." Nicola and Lawrie were vague on this point, but they looked as intelligent as possible.

"But you won't say anything to people about what Lawrie said," urged Nicola. "They might—well—you know—they might think we were conceited—and we're not. We just—it's only because—" she floundered unhappily.

"I won't tell," said Tim. "'Crorse me 'eart an' 'ope to die.'" It sounded trustworthy.

"Thank you," said Nicola. "Lawrie does talk an awful lot."

"I don't," said Lawrie indignantly. "Nothing *like* as much as you. You know perfectly well, Nicola, that only last week Father said—"

"All right," said Nicola hurriedly. "I don't suppose Tim's a bit interested."

"Where are your family?" asked Tim tactfully. "I'd like

20

to look at them from a discreet distance."

"Second compartment up. Kay and Ann are by the windows and Rowan and Gin this end. Kay and Rowan have their backs to the engine 'cos they don't get sick in trains."

"I don't expect head girls do," said Tim, amused. She strolled off to look.

It was obviously the same family. They all had the same fair hair and blue eyes, although the others, except Karen, had curly hair, which Ann wore in plaits and Rowan and Ginty in short crops. Tim strolled nonchalantly past the compartment and back again.

"And very nice too," she remarked. "I'm glad to have seen the famous Marlows at last."

They looked at her doubtfully.

"You're teasing," said Lawrie at last.

"A little," agreed Tim candidly. "I think it's just a scrap funny to be so frightfully much esteemed. You don't mind, do you? Are there any more at home?"

"Not at home," said Nicola a little stiffly. "There's Giles and Peter. But they're away now."

"Where do they come in? And what do they do?"

"Giles is the eldest. He's in the Navy. And Peter comes between us and Ginty. He's at Dartmouth," said Nicola briefly. She still felt rather sore.

"I like the Navy," said Tim. She grinned at Nicola with her friendliest expression. "I like the Navy better than anything."

Thawing, Nicola grinned back. "So do I. Do you know—"

"*No*," interrupted Lawrie. "*Please* don't talk Navy now. *Please*, Tim. If you lived in our family you'd want a rest from it too, sometimes. When Giles comes home, Nick always wants to know what he's done every single minute he's been away. And then she wants to tell me all about it. It isn't that I don't quite like the Navy; but I do get tired of having it all the time."

"All right," said Tim sadly. "Only it's rather hard on

21

me if I'm going to be in the Third Remove and probably never speak to you again because you're in IIIA. Never mind. Have some chocolate."

She tugged a large bag out of her coat pocket and offered it. "We may as well finish all we can," she added with her mouth full, "because I don't suppose we're allowed to keep sweets. Unless I can persuade anyone that as I'm Aunt Edith's niece I ought to be allowed to keep them. I shall try, anyway." She looked into the bag and added: "But I expect it would be *safer* to eat them now."

They munched steadily, occasionally flattening themselves against the partition as other and unknown members of Kingscote passed up and down the train, looking for their friends. One tall dark girl smiled and gave them a lordly: "Hello, twins," before disappearing into the Marlow compartment.

Lawrie choked and blushed.

"Who's that?" asked Tim.

"That's Margaret Jessop. She's the games captain. She stayed with Kay on holiday," said Lawrie, blushing more deeply still.

"Lawrie's awfully keen on her," explained Nicola unnecessarily. "She's all right, you know. Quite matey."

"She won't be matey at school," protested Lawrie hurriedly, "and you can't expect it, Nicola."

"I don't," said Nicola calmly. "Is that the last piece, Tim? Because if so, you'd better have it as it's your bag."

"All right," said Tim. She put the square of chocolate into her mouth, squashed the bag into a ball and lowered the window to throw it out.

"Let's leave it down," said Nicola. "It's awfully stuffy."

"Mother said—" began Lawrie.

"We're not leaning out," Nicola forestalled her. "Mother didn't mean we were to suffocate. What time is it now?"

"Twenty to four," said Lawrie. "Look, Tim. This was my parting present."

"Super," said Tim. "Haven't you got one, Nick?"

A Knife with Sixteen Blades

"No," said Nicola proudly. "I've got a knife. Look. Sixteen blades *and* a corkscrew *and* a file *and* a thing for taking things out of horses' hooves—"

She handed the knife to Lawrie to pass to Tim. As she did so, the train rounded a curve, swinging them all against the farther side of the corridor.

"Ow!" cried Lawrie in anguish, as she knocked her knee. "That hurt."

"My knife!" cried Nicola in sudden horror. "You dropped it! I saw you!" She pushed Lawrie out of the way and leaned out of the carriage window, her hair blowing wildly in the wind. "It's on the step," she gasped. "Look!"

Leaning over her shoulders, the other two looked down. There was the knife, jigging a little with the motion of the train, and quite out of reach.

Tim said hopefully: "P'rhaps it'll stay there till the train stops and we can get it . . . . "

They watched in silence. The knife jigged a little this way and that; sometimes nearly over the edge, then back against the train. It seemed as though Tim might be right.

"Look out," cried Lawrie suddenly. "There's a tunnel! Nick!"

They pulled in their heads sharply.

"Oh quick," groaned Nicola to the express. "Do hurry, you beast. Quick, quick, quick."

There had never been so long a tunnel. Evil-smelling darkness filled the corridor. Tim wrinkled her nose, but did not care to suggest that they should close the window. Nicola stamped angrily. "Oh, do hurry, you—you *goods* train!"

The tunnel wall lightened, showed daylight. Another moment, and they were in the sunshine. Nicola's head went through the window.

"It's gone," she said after a moment in a too-calm voice "It's fallen off."

"In an emergency," Commander Marlow was given to

telling his family, "act at once." On occasion he amplified this, saying that it was also necessary to think clearly and sensibly and not to act on impulse. Nicola, however, had absorbed only the dictum that she was to act immediately. Before Tim or Lawrie realized what she was about she had ducked back into the corridor and pulled the communication cord.

A bell began to jangle. The train slowed. Nicola tugged at the door-handle, jerked it down, and leapt out on to the permanent way. A moment later she was racing back into the tunnel.

In the unexpected silence the sound of voices began to rise all along the train. Compartment doors were pushed back, and people looked out, asking one another what had happened. With the automatic reaction of authority to anything unusual, Karen and Margaret Jessop emerged from the Marlow compartment with Rowan, curious but unconcerned, at their heels. The queries promptly flowed in Karen's direction.

"What's happened, Karen?"

"Is there a breakdown?"

"Who pulled the communication cord?"

"Is someone ill?"

"I haven't the least idea," said Karen calmly. "I don't suppose it's anything at all, and you may just as well go back and sit down and stop fussing."

"Ooo! Karen! There's a door open! Look! Someone's fallen out! They must have! *Look*, Karen!"

Karen turned sharply and saw her young sister Lawrie and another child she had never seen before clinging on to the jamb of an open door while they stared down the line with startled and slightly open-mouthed expressions. Nicola was nowhere to be seen.

Karen's usual air of calm authority over all events vanished. She strode across to Lawrie and said in a sharp, shaken voice:

"Lawrie! What's happened? Where's Nick?"

Lawrie, confused by the rapidity of Nicola's actions and

Karen's frightened voice, became speechless. Karen shook her arm.

"What's *happened*, Lawrie?"

The guard, striding down the train, came to a stop by the open door.

"What's happened, miss? Has there been an accident? Who pulled that cord?"

"We don't know," said Margaret Jessop, since Karen was clearly incapable of answering. "Lawrie, can't you—"

"*Lawrie*," cried Karen despairingly. "Did you pull it? Has Nicola—? For goodness' sake—!"

"I *didn't*," panted Lawrie. "Don't *pinch*, Kay."

The rest of the carriage looked on, amused, puzzled or apprehensive. Someone began to giggle nervously.

"There's Nick," said Tim's cool voice. She pointed up the line. No one had asked her any questions and she saw no reason to volunteer information. Probably Nicola would prefer to tell her own story. But there was no reason why she should not call attention to a perfectly obvious fact.

Nicola, looking grimy but cheerful, emerged from the tunnel. The guard strode off to meet her. The colour returned to Karen's face. She was so angry with Nicola that had she been within reach she would have slapped her. She watched in silence, standing on the step, as Nicola and the guard met. Nicola beamed at him, talking earnestly. His back, thought Karen, did not look as though he were mollified by her explanation. The voices of the deeply interested school, hanging out of the windows, came to her quite clearly.

"Who is it?"

"New, isn't she?"

"She looks like Kay Marlow."

"There can't be *more* of them."

"Yes, there are. Look, there's another little one by Karen."

"They must be twins."

"Did she fall out?"

"Was it a dare?"

And then behind her came Ginty's clear voice from the compartment. "Has Nick fallen out? Well, I can't *see*, Ann. What *has* she done, then?"

"Oh, you shut up, for goodness' sake," muttered Karen to herself.

A lean, tweed-clad lady hurried past.

"That would happen," said Margaret softly. "Never a disaster, but Ironsides is on the spot."

Karen said nothing, digging her hands down into the pockets of her blazer. Nicola, standing between the guard and Miss Cromwell, looked small and slightly alarmed.

The guard strode back past the open door, looking stiff and annoyed. Nicola, in Miss Cromwell's keeping, was brought up a moment later. Still in silence, Karen reached down a hand and pulled her into the corridor; together, and with more ceremony, Karen and Margaret helped Miss Cromwell up on to the step. Miss Cromwell climbed into the corridor and slammed the carriage door. The train began to move.

On principle, Miss Cromwell did not approve of prefects. She gave as her reasons that their duties interfered with scholarship work, and that their so-called responsibilities made them conceited and altogether above themselves. Where another mistress would have allowed the episode to rest until they reached school and a certain amount of privacy, Miss Cromwell attacked immediately, being of the opinion that bubbles of conceit required pricking hard and often.

"Well, Karen. What one might, I think, call a most unfortunate beginning to the term."

The crowd in the corridor, who liked Karen, but were never averse to seeing authority in trouble, stayed to listen.

Karen said nothing.

"I should have thought that any senior with sense, let alone a senior who is, supposedly, entrusted with some responsiblity, would have seen to it that a silly little girl was not allowed to roam at will, amusing herself by inconveniencing us all."

"I didn't know—" began Karen, low-voiced.

"My dear Karen," said Miss Cromwell, "it's your business to know. If you are unable to control your own family, I fail to see how you can expect to have any authority over the rest of the school."

Karen, scarlet-faced, said nothing. Rowan and Margaret exchanged a quick, angry glance.

"If Nicola is so childish and undisciplined, she should not have been allowed to play alone in the corridor. Stopping a train for no good reason is a very serious matter. I feel sure that Miss Keith will take a very grave view of the whole affair. As to the fine—"

"Father will pay the fine, naturally," said Rowan in a gentle, courteous voice. Unlike Karen, she did not find sarcasm particularly disconcerting. So she spoke politely and smiled pleasantly at Miss Cromwell, as though they shared a joke.

"I'll pay it," cried Nicola. "Well, I will, Rowan. I've saved—"

Rowan trod quietly, but heavily, on her foot. Nicola relapsed into silence.

"Who will and who will not pay will be a matter for Miss Keith to decide. I shall report the whole affair to her as soon as we return and I trust that you, Karen, will hold yourself in readiness to see her whenever she sends for you."

"Yes, Miss Cromwell," said Karen. Her voice shook slightly.

"Everyone will return to her compartment," said Miss Cromwell, satisfied that Karen had had enough. The crowd began to melt, casting sympathetic glances at Karen and amused smiles at Nicola. "Karen—can you manage this child for the remainder of the journey, or must I sit with your family for you?"

Karen gasped.

"We can manage, thank you, Miss Cromwell," said

Rowan in the same composed voice. She took Nicola by the shoulder and pushed her gently in the direction of their compartment. Margaret Jessop had vanished unobtrusively and the Marlow family was left alone to sort itself out.

There was a long silence.

"I say, Karen," began Nicola nervously.

"Oh, be quiet," said Karen, an odd tremor in her voice. "You make me tired. Always rushing around in a state of wild excitement and never stopping to think." She hunched her shoulders and looked out of the window. The others looked at her apprehensively. They knew from long experience that Karen, who seemed as a rule calm and matter-of-fact, could be thrown off-balance as easily as Lawrie by sudden and unexpected disaster. Karen knew it too; and she was uncertain, this time, how well she had managed to conceal those moments of panic when she thought Nicola had been hurt, possibly killed. Not very well, she thought miserably; and it had been Rowan who had stood up to Ironsides, while she herself blushed and stammered like any junior—

"I must tell Peter," burst out Ginty irrepressibly. "He's always been absolutely wild to pull a communication cord or smash one of those things that stop escalators—"

"Be *quiet*, Ginty," snapped Karen, without looking round.

"You needn't bite my head off," retorted Ginty. "For once I haven't done a thing."

"Oh, Gin, for heaven's sake," said Rowan. "don't talk as though you were the tomboy of the Remove. All through the holidays you kept trying to give the impression that a mild case of bounds-breaking had brought you to the edge of expulsion. I could have throttled you."

"There was a row," said Ginty indignantly. "An awful row. Miss Keith said—"

"I know you went round weeping for days after whatever Miss Keith said," said Rowan pitilessly, "but that still doesn't make you the naughtiest girl in the Fourth."

Ginty turned scarlet. "I *didn't* cry."

"All right," said Rowan. "You didn't cry. It was an extraordinary coincidence that just that week you had such a very bad cold. Now dry up, do."

"Actually," said Lawrie to Ginty, ignoring Rowan because it was so extremely mean to let people know that you knew when they'd been crying, "actually Miss Keith doesn't think anything like that at all. She thinks—what was it, Nick?—that you're rather wild but that you've got a lot of good stuff in you."

Ginty gaped.

"What on earth are you talking about?" demanded Rowan. "How do you know what Miss Keith thinks?"

"I do," said Lawrie loftily. "I do. That's all."

"I suppose," said Karen acidly, "she just happened to stroll past and give you her impressions of the family?"

"No," said Lawrie nonchalantly. "But we do know what she thinks. Don't we, Nick? We have it on—on the very best authority."

Nicola smiled faintly. "Yes."

"How?" demanded Rowan curtly.

"Shall we tell them?" asked Lawrie of Nicola.

But Nicola was feeling too apprehensive of disgrace to play the game of tantalizing properly.

"We were talking to her niece," she said flatly. "She told us."

"Oh, Nick!" cried Lawrie, disappointed.

"Her niece?" said Rowan, with much the same incredulity with which Nicola had remarked "An aunt?"

"She's twelve and a half and she's going to be in the Third Remove," elaborated Nicola. "And her name's Tim. At least, it's Thalia actually. Thalia Keith."

"Why Tim because her name's Failure?" puzzled Ann.

"That's what Lawrie thought it was. But it isn't Failure. It's Thalia. A muse or something."

"Was she the child standing with Lawrie by the door?" asked Karen curtly.

Nicola subsided. "I—expect so, Kay."

A gloomy silence fell on the compartment. For the moment, they had all, except Karen, forgotten that Nicola had stopped the train.

"Ironsides is always a beast," murmured Ann hesitantly at length. "And people do *know* she always likes to bite the prefects. It's one of her things."

"But she doesn't always have the opportunity to do it so publicly," snapped Karen, exasperated, "and not usually with such good reason. And I've still got to see Keith and she'll think, naturally, that I'm a perfect imbecile."

"Why?" breathed Nicola.

"Because if it's your family, the staff always think you ought to be able to see out of the back of your head. If it had been any other junior it would have been *her* fault, unless I'd been actually standing beside her. As it's you—well, naturally, I should have known by instinct."

Nicola and Lawrie looked at one another guiltily from beneath dropped lashes.

"You look a perfect sight," added Karen crossly, and turned again to stare out of the window.

"You do rather," said Ann more gently. "Turn round and let me tidy you up a bit. How on earth did you get so filthy?"

"I expect it was the tunnel," said Nicola, licking Ann's handkerchief meekly.

"But what—why were you *in* the tunnel? Why did you pull the cord?"

"My knife," said Nicola reluctantly, her eyes on Karen's averted head. "It fell out. I couldn't help it, Ann."

"I dropped it," murmured Lawrie. "It was an accident, honestly."

"That knife," said Karen viciously. "I've a good mind to take it away altogether."

"You can't," cried Nicola. "It's my parting present. You can't!" And they sat gazing furiously at one another, their expressions oddly alike.

The train slowed: slowed and stopped. They had arrived.

Karen sprang up and pulled her suitcase down from
the rack.

"I'm going up by taxi," she said abruptly, abandoning
the careful arrangements of the previous night, when
they had decided that the four youngest should ride,
since Ann was perfectly capable of ushering the twins
into Miss Keith's room before they unpacked. "If I can see
Keith before Ironsides does, I will. But I'm not having
Nicola along. She can walk up with you, Rowan, and
arrive when things have cooled down. And besides,"
added Karen honestly, "I'm not owning her in that
blouse. Everyone we pass will say: *That's* the child who
stopped the train. They must be related."

"All right," agreed Rowan calmly. She lifted the
suitcases down from the rack and saw Lawrie and Nicola
safely on to the platform.

"Rowan," whispered Nicola.

"What?"

"*Will* they know from my blouse?"

"Not if you put your blazer on," said Rowan coolly,
handing it to her. "Don't bother Kay just now. She's in
one of her flaps."

Nicola struggled thankfully into her blazer. Even so,
she felt unhappily conspicuous as she followed Rowan
meekly to the taxi and handed her suitcase to be stowed
on the roof. People turned to look at her and say:

"She *is* a Marlow—Must be, she's with Rowan—Why
did she?—Was she ill?—Perhaps she was trying to run
away—Wasn't Ironsides in a bate?"

The taxi containing the rest of the family moved off.
Rowan, who seemed unmoved by either glances or voices,
spoke over her shoulder and said: "Come on, infant."

They turned out of the station with its beds of asters
and nasturtiums and went up the High Street, Nicola
running a few steps every now and then in order to keep
level with Rowan. They had passed the grey bulk of the
cathedral which reared up in the centre of the city,
making the new shops which faced it across the spread of

grass look small and flimsy, before Nicola ventured a careful:

"Rowan?"

"'M?"

"Is it a very awful thing to have done?"

"It's not the most sensible thing the family's ever pulled out of the hat."

"They couldn't—Miss Keith wouldn't expel me, would she?"

"Send you back by return of post and say you weren't what she was expecting? No, I shouldn't think so."

Nicola looked relieved. "You know, Rowan, I don't honestly see what else I could have done."

"Don't you, now?"

"No, Rowan, honestly."

"Well, I don't see what else you could have done to get the knife back. The only other thing you could have done would have been to say: Well bless my soul. It's gone."

"Just lose it?"

"Yes."

"*Rowan!*"

"I suppose it never struck you, did it, my pretty, that another train might run into us from behind if we pulled up unexpectedly? I don't say it would. I say *might*, not knowing how railways arrange these things. Or, of course, that while you were skipping footloose in the tunnel, a train might have come the other way and squashed you flat?"

"Do you mean I might have been *killed*?" said Nicola incredulously.

"It does come within the bounds of possibility." Rowan looked down at Nicola sardonically. "Not, of course, that any of us would mind much. What's one more or less in a family our size?"

"Well!" said Nicola, flabbergasted. She was silent for quite five minutes; then as they turned into a teashop, she found tongue to ask where they were going and why.

"So that you can get a little cleaner than is possible

with handkerchief and lick. You don't need to arrive at
school looking more conspicuous than necessary."

Nicola found herself in the cloakroom at the back of the
shop. Looking in the mirror she found that there was a
good deal of dirt which Ann had only managed to move
from the centre of her face to the outside rim. Rowan,
leaning easily against the row of basins, directed oper-
ations.

"That's better," she said at last, flicking at the tail of
Nicola's skirt which had become unaccountably covered
with whitewash. "You look quite human now. Put on a
clean blouse before you see Keith and she'll probably
think the whole thing was a product of Ironsides'
imagination. And if she should refer to it, just lie low and
say, Yes, Miss Keith, and No, Miss Keith, at the
appropriate moments."

"Yes, Rowan," said Nicola meekly.

"I'll stand you a drink if you like," added Rowan
handsomely as they went back into the shop. "Orange,
Lemon, or Raspberry?"

Since she had never tried it before, Nicola chose
Raspberry. Her legs dangling from the high stool,
sucking Raspberryade through a straw, she began to feel
less uneasy.

"You'd better have a sundae too," said Rowan thoughtfully. "You can't be taken out more than once in a term
by a senior, so we may as well make the most of it now
we're here."

Nicola agreed enthusiastically.

"I had chocolate on the train," she said, studying the
card with concentration, "and I'm drinking Raspberry
now, so I think I'll have a peach sundae, please, Rowan."

"I suppose you can follow your own reasoning," said
Rowan idly. "Was it the niece who provided the chocolate?
Tim or Failure or whatever her name is?"

"Thalia," protested Nicola. "Yes, it was."

"Which reminds me. Did she really tell you what Miss
Keith had said about us, or was Lawrie being funny?"

Nicola grinned.

"No, she really did. D'you want to know what she said about you?"

Rowan considered.

"On the whole, not, I think. My relationship with Miss Keith is what you might call delicately balanced on a razor edge of mutual toleration. I wouldn't like to do anything to upset it."

"But it was perfectly all right, Rowan. It's quite a thing you'd like said."

"Then definitely not. I should blush every time I met her. And I think it might be as well—we did warn you and Lawrie, didn't we, not to go round spouting things Kay and I might have said about people?"

"Yes, you did. Lots of times."

"Well, tell Keith's niece from me that it would be just as well if she didn't run round school saying: Aunty says—in a loud, clear voice."

Nicola murmured noncommittally through a mouthful of peach and ice-cream. Probably Rowan was right. But for some reason, she didn't see herself telling Tim any such thing. She swallowed the lump of peach and asked Rowan politely about the state of the netball team.

Presently, replete and amicable, they strolled through the remainder of the town and out along the wood-fringed road to the school. It was all more or less familiar to Nicola, who had come down quite often with her parents and Lawrie to Speech Days and end of term plays, and had strolled, shy but proud, about the pleasant flowery garden, watching the quick, admiring glances flung at Karen and Rowan when the juniors thought they weren't looking. But it was a new and different feeling to be wearing the school uniform herself: and though she was still pleased and excited to be coming to Kingscote at last, she did wish, uneasily, that she had not started her school career by stopping a train; and when at last they turned in at the school gates and walked up the drive to the big white stucco-fronted building, her heart bumped so hard that she thought Rowan would probably notice and tell her to sit down until it stopped.

Hall and stairs and landing were crowded with people passing to and fro, or standing in small gossipy groups, as Rowan and Nicola went in. Nicola, feeling very new and shy, kept closely behind Rowan and wished Lawrie were with her to share the feeling. She was glad that when people hailed Rowan, as they seemed to do continuously, Rowan only waved and did not stop. They had nearly reached the top of the stairs before a thin, brown-haired girl said in a voice which Nicola recognized with a shock as not friendly at all:

"Well, if it isn't our Rowan come back."

"So it is," said Rowan. "How observant of you." Her voice was not friendly either.

"And you've brought two more back with you, they tell me. Two more of your illustrious family to bring honour to the dear old school."

Rowan looked cool and pleasant.

"Somebody has to," she observed politely. "If you will insist on leaving it to us, we have to do our best."

"And one of them stopped the train, I hear. Such a clever and original way of making the Marlows conspicuous the very first day."

"What a shame you didn't think of it first," countered Rowan swiftly and ran on up the stairs.

"Who was that?" gasped Nicola when they were out of earshot.

"Lois Sanger," said Rowan briefly.

"The one you had the row with?"

"I've told you before, Nicola, that you're to forget the things we told you before we knew you were coming here."

"I'm only saying it to you," said Nicola, injured. "I don't even know what the row was."

"Then forget it. That's Miss Keith's door. I won't go in with you. It looks so elderly. Just knock and await developments."

She smiled briefly before she walked away, but she still sounded curt and angry. Nicola sighed and looked sadly at Miss Keith's door. It was a pity Rowan was cross. She would have preferred to have had someone with her to say, This is Nicola. But she supposed the longer she waited the worse she would feel. She knocked carefully and was told to come in.

Miss Keith had not been particularly pleased by Karen's story, but she had not said a great deal. Like Miss Cromwell, she had suggested that it had been unwise to allow Nicola and Lawrence to stand unattended in the corridor; and, after a pause, had remarked that she would have to consider making a rule forbidding any junior to run about the train corridors unless travelling with her parents.

Karen murmured: "Yes, Miss Keith," and looked fixedly at an upturned corner of leather on Miss Keith's blotter.

"And I think, perhaps, that as Nicola is new this term, it would be better if you were to write to your father about the fine. I should be sorry to have to make an official school matter of something which has happened almost before Nicola is a member of the school."

"Yes, Miss Keith."

"Of course, had Nicola been here longer, I should have had to take a very different attitude. That type of impulsive action can have the most serious consequences, and not only for the person directly concerned. In this particular case, no actual harm did result. But at the same time, any members of the public who were travelling on the train will carry away a very bad impression of the way our girls behave."

"Yes."

"Your family has had a very good record here, Karen; and I should be sorry if that record were to be spoiled, particularly sorry if it were to be spoiled while you are head girl. But I'm sure it isn't necessary for me to remind you that Nicola and Lawrence must be treated exactly like any other juniors and if such a thing were to occur again I should have to consider very seriously whether I could allow Nicola to remain here."

"Yes."

"Very well, Karen. I will have a word with Nicola when she arrives. After that, unless she continues to be troublesome, we had better all forget the whole unfortunate business."

That was that, and Karen removed herself, feeling depressed and humiliated. Had Miss Keith called her back to say that she had decided that Val Longstreet should be head girl, she would have felt dejected but not surprised. She wondered, as she ran up the stairs to her own room, whether her father, also, would think she should have foreseen that Nicola would drop her knife and hold up the Southern Region in consequence.

To Nicola, Miss Keith repeated much of what she had said to Karen, adding that she hoped Nicola would do nothing so foolish again, but settle down to be a good, useful member of society. Nicola said: "Yes, Miss Keith," for the last time, and whisked thankfully out of the study, shutting the door very gently behind her. The prefect who stood at the end of the passage with a list in her hand, ticked off her name and told her that she would be in Dormitory Six, first on the right at the top of the stairs.

"You're lucky to be so many," she added with a friendly smile. "It's much the nicest of the sisters' rooms. And did you really stop the train, or is that a rumour?"

Nicola said No, she really had, and fled upstairs to find the white door with the black six on it. Rowan, Ann, Ginty and Lawrie were there already, Ginty stuffing the clothes from her trunk into a drawer and Ann unpacking in a calm, tidy way for Lawrie. As Nicola came in Rowan was remarking lazily:

"You'll have to put all that tidy before you go down, Gin, so you might as well do it first as last."

"I don't see why," protested Ginty. "We're a sisters'

room, so we can't do anything for the Dorm Prize, so I don't see that it matters."

"Shocking outlook," said Rowan calmly. "The point is, my dear Virginia, that Matron will inspect your drawers just the same as anyone else's, and if they're not tidy she'll come to me about it. And I can't be bothered with little idiocies of that kind."

Ginty sat back on her heels, and pushed the hair out of her eyes.

"You are a bossy beast, Rowan. I do think Kay's lucky to have a room to herself."

"When you're head girl, you'll have a room to yourself too," said Rowan, unmoved. "In the meantime, you can at least *start* with your drawers tidy, whatever happens to them in a week's time."

"Hullo, Nicky," said Ann. "That's your cubicle. I'll unpack for you as soon as I've finished Lawrie's."

"I can do it myself, thank you," said Nicola quickly; she was sometimes irritated by Ann's unfailing good-nature. "I s'pose I can't be by the window, can I, Rowan?"

"No, you can't," said Rowan, who seemed to have recovered her temper. "That's reserved for your respected seniors, meaning me and Ann. How did you get on?"

"All right," said Nicola, kneeling down to tug at the straps of her trunk. "No, don't *bother*, Ann. I can do it myself."

She plunged into her unpacking, stowing her things away in frantic haste to be finished before Ann could come to her assistance. When everything was in place, she sat back on her heels and carefully unwrapped the two photographs allowed by regulation and put them tenderly on top of her dressing-chest. One was of the ship in which Giles was serving, the other a reproduction of Abbot's portrait of Nelson which Giles had bought for her at the National Portrait Gallery.

"It would show nicer feeling, Nicky dear," commented Rowan, "if you had Giles instead of his ship and possibly an expensively framed cabinet portrait of Father and

Mother instead of Nelson. Don't you think so, Ann?"

Nicola grinned, but said nothing. She was far too used to being teased about Nelson and the Navy to trouble to argue. She sauntered over to the window and stood beside Rowan, looking out.

"We can see the cathedral from here," she remarked.

"You can see it from everywhere," said Ann. "You can't get lost round here. You only have to look for the spire and make for that."

"And the sea!" cried Nicola unheeding. "Oh, look, Rowan. There's the sea!"

"It always is there," said Rowan, unmoved. "Has been for years."

"That girl was right about it being the nicest dorm," said Nicola contentedly, hanging out of the window. "I wish we didn't have this silly stuff with roses on it, though," she added, flicking the window curtains.

"I suppose you'd like a nice grey chintz printed with battleships," retorted Ginty, slamming the last drawer of a surprisingly tidy chest tight shut. "Well, I'm going to see if Monica's back. So long."

She went out, banging the door behind her. Someone shouted from the gravel path below. Nicola waved back.

"There's Tim," she said. "Come on, Lawrie. You must be ready by now. Let's go down."

Lawrie looked doubtfully at Ann.

"That's all right," said Ann, who was still filling Lawrie's drawers in a slow, methodical fashion. "You run along. I'll finish this."

The twins collided in the doorway, glared at one another impatiently and then rushed downstairs to the garden.

"Quite at home already," said Lois Sanger dryly as Lawrie passed her at full speed with an inch to spare. "I always feel it must be so gratifying to be a Marlow."

This is the beginning of Autumn Term, *the first of Antonia Forest's series of stories about the Marlows. To*

A Knife with Sixteen Blades

find out what happened to Nicola and Lawrie at Kingscote, you can read Autumn Term *and its sequels,* End of Term, The Cricket Term *and* The Attic Term.

The Trouble with Donovan Croft

<><><><><><><><><><><><><><><><><><><><><><><><><><><><><><><><><>

Bernard Ashley

Keith Chapman's parents are fostering Donovan Croft. On the first day of term, Donovan goes to school with Keith.

Small groups of children stood about like strangers in the playground. There was little of the charging about and booting of balls that went on during most playtimes and before school. On the first day of the school year everyone was slightly apprehensive. The new fourth-years, now the senior group and cocks of the walk, showed the most activity, greeting one another with loud shouts and over-enthusiastic thumps on the back. The rest were very quiet, adjusting to being back in school at all, and taking care of new trousers and frocks. But the quietest clusters of all, here and there attended by older brothers, sisters and the occasional mum, were the new first-years, last

41

year's top infants who were now very much at the bottom
of the pile. They resembled young deer on the edge of the
herd, unsure and frightened but with heads held high.

Every so often a teacher walked through the playground, to be greeted in varying fashions by the different
groups. The new fourth-year children rarely deigned to
speak to other than fourth-year teachers, whom they
greeted with loud and polite explosions of welcome and
wide smiles. There were two or three new young
teachers, ignored by all but the few children who rushed
to talk to any adult, and both popular and unpopular
teachers who walked through to clamorous attention or
to total disregard. Mr Bryan was mobbed from gate to
steps by all but the fourth-years, while Mr Henry might
as well have been walking across a beach at midnight.
Mr Roper was already in the building, having been
welcomed shortly after eight o'clock by a few shivering
individuals whose parents had gone to work early and
turned them out at the same time.

Class members greeted each other after the six-week
break in different ways. Some had seen a lot of their
particular friends in the holiday, and there wasn't much
new to say. Others, not living so close together, welcomed
their classmates with restrained delight, everyone talking and no one listening. Nobody spoke to Shemem
Parveen, the brightly-clad Pakistani girl with spiteful
fingers, nobody ever did; while Paul Wicks, the football
captain who held a place in the District Side even in his
third year, was met on all sides by warm disciples.
Groups of friends, who played together for different
reasons, were reunited. The older "dinner children"
formed a tight band, allowing in a few of the sandwich-
bringers as hangers on. Children who went home to
dinner made up their own gangs, and those who lived
near to one another, or who crossed the road together
with the lollipop man, somehow stuck together in the
playground. All sorts of reasons brought different children together.

There seemed to be little notice taken of anyone's colour; a good brain, a talented right foot or netball arm were what seemed to matter. The exceptions were the few Asian children who spoke poor English. They talked together in a fast foreign language by the school steps: the middle of the playground was not for them.

Keith led Donovan in through the Transport Avenue gate. This was Keith's usual gate, and if he ever missed Dave and Tony on the way to school they always met up here. Keith's eyes scanned the crowded playground for his two special friends. They had grown up through the school from the Infants together and they usually sought each other's company. It was an easy friendship, punctuated by thumps and scuffles, snorts and giggles. There were no rules, no special demands were made on one another except their company. It just seemed a natural grouping, like a small pack of dogs hunting together for a reason which none of them understood.

Dave and Tony were there, just inside the gate as usual. Keith saw them wave and heard the familiar shouts—"Wotcher Kee!" from Dave and "Over here!" from Tony. He grabbed Donovan's arm and tried to steer him over towards them. This was important. He badly wanted them all to get on well together. But as Keith turned round, he became, with Donovan, the focus of considerable attention, and he found his way to Dave and Tony barred by an inquisitive group of children from his year. A new boy in the third year was worth a glance or two.

"'Ere, Chapman, who's 'e?"

"Is he new?"

"There's another blackie."

"Another wog."

This form of attention was not new to Donovan. He had supposedly swung through the jungle of trees and eaten cat food ever since he first went to infant school with all the other five-year-olds in North London. His reaction now was to stare sullenly ahead with unfocused eyes.

Keith stopped pushing towards Dave and Tony for a
moment. He was going to have to say something before
he was allowed to get away.

"His name's Donovan. He's living with us. Any objec-
tions?"

Nobody objected. Only the older children dared to
challenge the strength of the triangle of friendship.
Keith and Donovan were now the centre of a little
throng. Any friend of Keith's was a friend of theirs, and
there was a certain warmth in the circle.

"Hope he's in our class."

"'Ere, mate, are you any good in goal?"

"Is your mum dead?"

The inquiries were necessary to fit Donovan into the
order of things, to help them decide their feelings about
him. Everyone has a place, and the sooner it is decided
and fixed the happier everyone is. Donovan remained
silent, so Keith tried to explain.

"His mum's gone back to look after his grandad."

"Where? Africa?"

"No, Jamaica. But Donovan's living at our house till
she gets back. He's, like, my foster-brother."

The words "foster-brother" carried sufficiently over the
gathered heads to reach the ears of Dave and Tony, alert
as ears always are to news which might affect the
hearers. Neither of the boys spoke, but the beginning of a
sneer wrinkled Dave's nose and a meaningful glance
passed between the two boys, now left standing on their
own.

The group round Keith and Donovan fell silent as they
took in the full meaning of the black boy being foster-
brother to Chapman.

"Foster-brother?" queried Len Andrews.

"Yes, foster-brother," replied Keith shortly, trying to
bring the questioning to an end. He'd had enough now
and wanted to meet up with Dave and Tony. He spelt it
out slowly. "He's my foster-brother."

"Is he?" said a voice from the throng. "Is that why you

don't want to know us any more?"

Keith swung round at the sound of the familiar voice. He knew before he looked that it was Dave.

"It must be nice having a little brown brother. Is he brown all over, Chapman? Is his bum as brown as his face?"

Suddenly Keith found it hard to breathe. His heart thumped and his chest went tight.

"Shut up, Dave," said Tony, who was standing with an arm round Dave's shoulder. "Don't be rotten."

"Well, I only wondered," said Dave. "I'm just interested, that's all."

He coloured a little before Keith's white, angry and betrayed stare.

"Watch it, Smith," Keith managed to hiss out, "or I'll put one on you!"

Dave broke away from the crowd.

"Oh, come on, Tone," he shouted. "Let's go. I'm scared stiff."

He suddenly swung back on Keith. "But I'll tell you, Chapman, when you get fed up with your brown brother don't come running back to be friends with us! If you're too busy for us today you can bloody stay like it!"

With a backward glance Tony followed Dave away, and some of the others went with them. A few minds were suddenly being changed as it became obvious that Keith could no longer draw strength from Tony and Dave.

"See you later," said one, not sure yet, as he drifted away. Keith and Donovan might make a formidable partnership on their own.

"Just don't forget your old mates, Chapman," said another, an emboldened boy who had never claimed Keith's friendship. Then someone at the back of the circle shoved everyone forward, but a heavy plastic ball kicked by one of the fourth-years landed in their midst and scattered the group, some to chase it and others to avoid the footballers, and the tension went out of the situation.

"Let them get on with it," said Winnie Marshall, one of

the few girls in the group. "What's it all about anyway, Keith?"

Keith pulled a face. "I dunno," he answered.

And truly, he didn't.

Mr Henry was on the whistle.

"Just my fortune on the first day of term," he had complained in the staffroom. "It needs one of the women to sort these blessed infants out."

Nevertheless, at five minutes to nine he stood on the stone steps which led from the playground into the lower hall and gave a long, shrill blow on his plastic whistle. The response was typical of the first day of term; it was immediate. Everyone stopped running, most stopped talking, and the assembled playground turned to face the school. Later on in the term it would be different: a series of whistlings and a variety of coaxes and threats would be necessary, especially by the younger teachers, before order was achieved. But now there was silence, and no movement. Wisely, Mr Henry decided to get rid of the likely source of trouble first. He pulled himself up to his full five feet seven, straightened his tweed jacket like an officer on parade, and bellowed his first order.

"I want all you new ones, you infants, to walk quietly into school and wait for Mrs Pressnose in the lower hall."

This lady's unfortunate name brought a relieved smile and a small titter to the new children as they walked forward to the steps. One of the first to reach them, a white-faced little girl with blonde pig-tails, suddenly presented Mr Henry with some flowers she had been carrying for her new teacher. He accepted them with a smile, then changed his stance to the "at ease" position, holding them out of sight behind his back.

One by one he called the classes into school by age until he reached his own third-year class. "My new class stand firm," he shouted, and then went on through the fourth-years to the end until thirty-odd individuals were left, scattered over the otherwise empty playground. A small bunch of mothers retreated to the gate, and the first fluttering sweet papers of the term chased about the tarmac. Mr Henry began to relax.

"Now, class 3H," he yelled, "advance to the steps and be recognized."

Slowly the children shuffled into a group beneath their new teacher. They stood looking up at him, apprehension on some of the faces; for the past week or so, as the new term drew nearer, they had wondered and worried about the notorious Mr Henry.

He was a scrupulously neat and tidy man. His thinning hair was brushed down flat, his neatly clipped military moustache treated like a pet. Above a pair of well-pressed cavalry twill trousers was a smart bright yellow squared waistcoat, and across it, marking the outer boundary of his ample stomach like a parade-ground chain, ran a long droopy silver Albert for his watch.

"Right, let's see what sort of squad we've got this year. Girls, advance to the bottom of the steps."

Silently the seventeen girls stepped forward. One or two, faces up and smiling, would soon be chattering themselves into the jobs of bringing his tea, changing his calendar, running his errands. But now they stood quietly like the rest, to be looked over. Mr Henry's trained military eye scanned from left to right.

"Yes, you look reasonably like human beings," he pronounced at last. There was a big, slightly forced, laugh from the whole class. "Now the boys; let's have a look at you. Up straight!"

The boys threw out their chests and stood to attention like a squad of raw recruits. Their faces were eager and shining. Old Henry didn't seem so bad after all, now that you got to know him.

"Good, good."

As yet he didn't know one from another, they were just his new class. Their paths might have crossed before, but he was ignorant of any names. Keith looked at Donovan out of the corner of his eye. Donovan's stance and expression had hardly changed since they first came into the playground. He stood with his feet together, his hands hanging down by his sides and his head slightly bowed, facing the steps. His eyes were open, but they were glazed and lifeless. Keith looked the other way, to where he knew Dave and Tony were standing. They were very close together, ready like the rest for a favour to fall from Mr Henry. Normally Keith would have been close too, part of the inseparable unit, but now he felt separated by more than a few metres between them. This wasn't at all how he had imagined the beginning of term.

"Well, I'll soon get to know your names, and your characters no doubt," Mr Henry went on. "All your strengths . . . " He paused, and then with greater emphasis, " . . . and all your little weaknesses." He looked around him and expanded his theme. "I'll get to know those who can't add, or can't read, or can't sit still, or can't get up in the morning, or can't do as they're told . . . "

His shafts found homes in various beating hearts as their "little weaknesses" were catalogued, but being old hands at the business of going to school, they gave nothing away by their faces.

"And now," concluded Mr Henry to everyone's relief, "we shall walk into the class-room in a quiet and orderly fashion, beginning the term as we mean to go on."

He turned abruptly and shouted at the door in front of him, bouncing his voice back to his troops behind:

"Follow me. Girls first, then the boys." And he marched into the darkened doorway, his posy clutched at forty-five degrees behind his back. Keith's sigh of relief as he went into school was especially heavy: perhaps because it was for two.

You can read the whole story of Keith and Donovan in The Trouble with Donovan Croft.

Seymour's Century

<><><><><><><><><><><><><><><><><><><><><><><><><><><><><><><><>

Jan Mark

There was one long seat running most of the way across the front of the top deck, then the gangway, then a sole unsociable seat, all by itself in the corner. There were two more like it, lined up in single file behind the first, to make room for the hole where the stairs went down, and after that the seats were in pairs and the passengers sat there, two by two. Heming, Seymour, Bracey and Ballard were not interested in sitting two by two, or one by one in the single seats. It was the front row they were after and they were prepared to go to desperate lengths to get it.

This was easy enough to achieve in the morning because they were the first people to get on the bus, and it rocked hollowly along the lanes for several miles before anyone else flagged it down. Afternoons were a different matter. The bus stopped right outside the school, but by the time it arrived it was already full. If they caught it outside Woolworth's there was more room, but they still could not depend on getting the front seat. The only way to secure that was to belt up Claygate, in at the back of Marks and Spencer's and out at the front, catercorner at the roundabout, through Boots where they were well known but not popular, across the traffic jam down St. Augustines and into the bus station.

Even then they might be beaten to it by the Snob Mob from the King's School, but most days they managed to reach the 705 stop before anyone else: anyone else who mattered, that was. There were plenty of other passengers at the head of the queue, old ladies mostly, as immovable as traffic bollards and not to be pushed around, but no one else who wanted the front seat. Even the Snob Mob didn't really want it, they just liked to keep the 705 Sports Club fuming impotently at the back until the bus reached Hay Heath, where the Snob Mob all got out. People from other schools smoked cigarettes on the bus. The Snob Mob smoked a cigar, one between the five of them, and held noisy debates about whether it was the done thing to take the band off first.

As a matter of fact, it was not even the front *seat* that they wanted. They were not particularly anxious to sit together for friendship's sake, for Heming disliked Bracey and Ballard despised Seymour, but they were prepared to sink their differences in the interests of the Sports Club, and what the Sports Club was after was the long metal ledge that ran right across the front of the bus, just below the window. At one end was the periscope that enabled the driver to look up from his cab below and observe misdeeds in the convex mirror that hung above it, but after that the ledge stretched away uninterrupted, with only a flat seam scross the middle; the centre line.

The Sports Club had begun by accident, one winter morning. Seymour had had words with Ballard at the bus stop, and was sitting away by himself in the corner, on one of the small seats, sulking over the maths homework that he hadn't done last night. Ballard, full of early morning malice, had begun flicking old bus tickets at him, rolled into sharp little balls, from the other end of the ledge. Seymour, who had his books spread out on the ledge, ignored the first half dozen missiles, but when one landed in the middle of his theorem he put down his pen and flicked it back to Ballard. Bracey intercepted and sent it down to Seymour's end, but Seymour pounced on it, tucked it under his thumb and ran his fingers along the ledge toward Ballard. Just in time Heming drew a goal post in the steam on the window, Seymour scored a try and Bracey converted it. Heming put the ball back on the centre line and drew a scoreboard on the front window. Ballard kicked off, Bracey raced to meet him and their hands met in a scrum of knuckles, surging up and down the ledge as fast as their fingers would carry them. Seymour hooked out the ball with his thumb and flicked it down the stair well. Heming booked him for wasting time and drew a grandstand on the left-hand window, full of grinning faces. Bracey drew floodlights. Heming found another bus ticket and play recommenced.

This time things were more orderly. Ballard and Seymour were the opposing teams, Bracey was the scorer and Heming was the ref. Seymour won by 29-8 and did not complete his maths homework. After the maths lesson, in which things were said, Heming booked him for bringing the game into disrepute.

On the way home, Seymour had another go at his maths homework and also finished his English essay, so that he could give his full attention to slaughtering Ballard next morning; but next morning Ballard turned up equipped with two matchsticks which he bent, near the ends, into neat little hooks, and a business-like sphere of silver paper with a ball-bearing inside it.

"Hockey today," said Ballard, putting the ball on the centre line. Seymour took the other matchstick and they bullied off. Seymour secured the ball and began dribbling but Ballard tripped him with a well-placed finger.

51

Heming booked Ballard and awarded Seymour a penalty flick. Bracey said the ball was lethal, especially to windows, and insisted that they went back to using bus tickets. Heming confiscated the ball-bearing and booked Ballard for bringing the bus into disrepair. Ballard said he hadn't, yet, and was going to appeal and Heming had better give him back his ball-bearing. Heming and Ballard then had an argument that lasted for the rest of the ride and the game was abandoned before half time. Ballard and Seymour agreed to finish it on the return journey, but were prevented from doing so by the presence of the Snob Mob and their cigar in the front seat. It was after this that the evening dash for the bus became a necessity and a habit.

The Sports Club became well established during the Spring Term. They played hockey in the mornings and football on the way home. The Snob Mob jeered openly but as Easter approached, Bracey pointed out that they were moving closer and closer to the front of the bus, and when play got really exciting they left their seats altogether and gathered round to watch. The Sports Club developed sinewy forearms and muscular fingers.

On the first day of the Summer Term they reassembled, having steered clear of each other throughout the holiday, and waited for Ballard to produce his two bent matches, but Ballard had a surprise for them. He brought out six matches, a lump of plasticine and an aniseed ball.

"Not even slightly sucked," said Ballard, rolling the aniseed ball up and down the playing field.

"What's all this, then?" said Heming, who had his notebook all ready to book Ballard.

"Cricket," said Ballard, setting up stumps, three at each end and stuck into the plasticine. "It's summer, isn't it?"

There was a slight snowstorm going on outside, but no one argued. After all, the Cup Final was over and done with so it must be summer. If they didn't get some cricket in quickly the summer would be over and the football season starting again.

"Ball looks a bit hard," said the cautious Bracey.

"But it's the right colour," said Ballard.

"Kerry Packer's team use a white one," said Heming.

"OK. OK. I'll suck it," said Ballard and put the ball in his mouth. When it came out again it was white and shiny. Ballard waved it about a bit to dry it out.

"We'll start with one-day matches," said Ballard. "Just to get our hands in. We should be ready for the First Test about half term."

The stumps were Swan Vestas. Bracey extracted one, struck it on the floor and set fire to a bus ticket.

"The Ashes," he said, replacing what was left of the stump. Heming booked him for damaging the pitch.

"Where's the bat?" said Seymour. "A matchstick'll never stand up to that ball."

"I thought of that," said Ballard, and took from his pocket an emery board. "My sister uses it for filing her nails, or her teeth, or something."

"It's got bits of your sister on it," said Heming.

"I made seventy-six not out with this, last night," said Ballard. "Left hand against right."

"I bet left hand was bowling," said Heming.

Ballard rolled the ball along the pitch and hit it with the emery board. It would have been a six but for the intervention of the window. There was a loud cracking sound and although the window did not break, Bracey became nervous and erected batting screens; an atlas at one end of the pitch and his history folder at the other. Seymour bowled, Ballard hit out for the boundary. The ball, still slightly moist, rolled through the Ashes and emerged looking like a truffle.

Seymour bowled again, Ballard swung wildly and Bracey just caught the ball as it was arcing towards the stair well. Hemming wrote *Ballard c Bracey b Seymour* and went into the outfield at the top of the stairs.

Then Seymour bowled to Bracey and scattered his stumps as Bracey got the bat jammed under his thumbnail. Heming wrote *Bracey tbw b Seymour*.

"What's that mean?" Bracey demanded, using the bat to file down his nail in case of a repetition.

"Thumb before wicket," said Heming.

Bracey took up the ball and bowled to Seymour. Seymour gave it a tentative pat and it trickled toward Bracey, then whizzed back again as the bus tilted into a double bend.

"Run, you fool," Heming cried as the bus took the second corner and the ball began its return journey.

"How? Where?" said Seymour, ready to race down the gangway.

"First two fingers," said Ballard, and Seymour began his dash for the other end, on the points of his nails, but he was run out by Bracey, sneaking up to the wicket, also on finger-tips and with the ball wedged between his knuckles. When stumps were drawn Bracey had made eight, Seymour five, Ballard twelve and Heming had been out for a duck four times. Ballard, whose hands were in training, had taken five wickets. Bracey, last man in, declared, and the game was resumed on the way home.

"How about a new ball?" said Seymour, looking at the old one which was by now pitted like an asteroid and would not roll. Ballard nipped off the bus to get another: a gob-stopper from the vending machine at the corner of the bus station. While he was gone the bus left without him. It passed him on the way out and after that the Sports Club caught entertaining glimpses of Ballard as he hurtled back through the city to intercept the bus outside Woolworth's. Bracey remarked that he had never seen Ballard move so fast. Heming said that when they got tired of cricket they could introduce track events. Seymour said yes, but the fact that Ballard was fast on his feet didn't mean that he was fast on his fingers and anyway, they could only do sprints on the window ledge. Ballard arrived at Woolworth's just in time to leap on the bus as the doors were closing. He staggered upstairs and tossed the ball on to the pitch. It was bright orange.

"Even Packer doesn't use an orange ball," said Heming.

"It was green when I bought it," Ballard gasped, sinking into his seat.

"Have you been sucking this one too?" said Heming, eyeing the glistening globe with distaste.

"I had to get the size down," said Ballard, self-righteously. "And I nearly choked, running with that thing in my mouth."

"I'll bring a marble tomorrow," said Seymour.

"Dodgy," said Bracey, setting up the screens again.

Seymour was first in, Ballard bowling. Heming retired to the stairs again and Bracey was wicket-keeper, point and silly mid-off; right hand, left hand and nose, respectively.

Seymour played a careful game and his score crept remorselessly toward double figures. Then the bus suddenly jerked to a halt at the level crossing and Seymour, off guard, hit out. The ball zipped straight past all of Bracey's fielders, missing silly mid-off by a millimetre, through Heming's unsuspecting fingers and away down the aisle between the seats.

"Get after it, man!" Bracey yelled, still quivering with shock. Heming recovered his wits and went after the ball. There was no sign of it. Heming fell to his knees and began looking under the seats, but it was not only seats that he had to contend with. The bus was full, and for every double seat there were four legs, duffle bags, briefcases, shopping baskets, a dog . . .

A dog.

Heming put his head under the seat and scanned the dog anxiously, but it showed no signs of having just eaten a cricket ball. However, it showed every sign of desiring to eat Heming. A bristly growl stirred it from snout to tail tip. Heming withdrew.

"Have you lost something?" asked the owner of the dog.

"A gob-stopper," said Heming, without thinking in advance how this might sound.

"A gob-stopper?" said the dog's owner. "Is it worth

looking for? It won't be exactly edible when you find it."

Heming decided against trying to explain and moved on, banging his head on the underside of the seat.

Two middle-aged women had overheard the conversation. "Fancy crawling about on the floor after a penny gob-stopper," said one, in a when-I-was-his-age sort of voice.

"You'd think boys from *that* school would be able to afford another one," said her friend. "I thought you had to pay to go to *that* school."

Heming recalled that he was in uniform, and that to be seen crawling about the top deck of a bus in pursuit of a gob-stopper would do nothing for the Good Name of the School, especially among the Snob Mob from King's, who were watching him with overt sneers. "Poor starving thing," said one, and dropped a crust to him, over the back of the seat. He would have to book himself for bringing the school into disrepute.

Meanwhile, at the front of the bus, Seymour had made thirty-three runs and was still going, although with flagging fingers.

"Can't I use my whole hand?" he pleaded.

"No," said the implacable Ballard. "I made seventy-six last night, I told you."

"Not all at once, I bet," said Seymour. "And I bet it was on a tablecloth. Thirty-seven."

Heming looked plaintively over Bracey's shoulder. "I can't find it. Make him declare."

"I declare. I declare!" said Seymour, gratefully. "Forty-one."

"No you don't," said Bracey, brutally. "Go and have another look. It must be up here somewhere."

Heming went to the rear of the bus, on all fours again. It was amazing how much rubbish had accumulated under the seats during the day. He found half a packet of Tunes and ten pence, which normally would have made him very happy, but not today. Fumbling in the dark he put his hand on a woman's leg and she kicked him; with good reason, Heming thought, looking at his filthy sticky hands. He was beginning to attract an unwelcome amount of attention, but not so much attention as the cricket match was. The whole of the Snob Mob had risen to its feet and crowded up to the boundary, chanting in unison, " . . . sixty-eight . . . sixty-nine . . . seventy!" Two or three total strangers had joined in urging Seymour towards his century.

"I'm going to declare," said Seymour, buckling at the knuckles. "Get me a brandy. Take me home to Mother. I can't go on."

"Yes you can," said Bracey. Ballard fought his way through the spectators and joined Heming. He flung himself full length on the floor and began scything under the seats with outstretched arms. "Get a move on, Heming," he said. "Seymour's wiping the floor with us."

"He needn't bother," said Heming. "We're doing all right by ourselves . . . Hey!"

The bus had stopped on the steep slope of Hay Heath and people were climbing over them to reach the stairs. Simultaneously, something else started to leave, as well. Down the aisle, covered in fluff, came the cricket ball. Heming and Ballard hurled themselves at it but it trundled by, ricocheted off a passing boot and went downstairs. Heming was first on his feet, as Ballard fell over the dog, and plunged after it. He was just in time to see the door closing as the cricket ball rolled across the lower deck and left the bus. At the same moment there came a great shout from above, followed by a spattering of applause.

"What's going on up there?" said the driver. "Tell those lads to sit down or I'll be up and they'll be off."

The bus started. The ball was gone, the game was over. Heming ascended the stairs and encountered the entire Snob Mob on its way down, having become so engrossed in Seymour's century that they had forgotten to get off.

Seymour had broken a nail and swore that he was developing blisters. Bracey had banged his head on the window when the bus stopped. Ballard had been bitten by the dog and Heming booked them all, because he felt like it.

Next day Seymour brought along a pack of cards and they played Stud Poker, for matchsticks.

The Scar

<><><><><><><><><><><><><><><><><><><><><><><><><><><><><>

Margaret Biggs

I wake up early because it's Wednesday. It's light
through the curtains, but too early to get up. The birds
are singing—funny how they always sound happy. I lie
curled up under the duvet and ponder about the day ahead.

It's a high-spot day—that means, I shall see Mrs
Chadwick. She takes us for English Wednesday and
Friday. "Sheila—darling Sheila—" I mutter to myself,
into the pillow. Of course I never call her that when she's
around. I keep my head down, and hardly open my
mouth. I always feel so scared of looking stupid. Some of
the others, Pete in particular, jabber away to her. She
never minds us making a lot of noise, she's always
friendly and interested in what we say. I wriggle with
pleasure and love, thinking about her. Then I catch sight
of my arm, and as always feel desperate. I hate the sight

of it, and wish I need never see it again. I shove it under the duvet. The scar snakes up it deeply, jaggedly. It will never fade, I know it will always be there, and though I always wear long-sleeved shirts which cover up most of it, it goes right down across the back of my hand, red and twisted, and people always notice. Pete says it's not too bad, but he doesn't mean it, it's unspeakable, it makes me feel sick. I know it is, I hate it, I'd do anything to get rid of it.

It happened four years ago, that terrible night I still dream about sometimes, and wake up sweating and rolling about in anguish, when we got tangled up with a juggernaut on the motorway, and Dad got killed, and Mum and I both got hurt, and Dan asleep in the back was all right, lucky devil. It's all a jumble in my mind of noise and horror and blaring horns and screeching sirens, sticky blood all over my shirt, and then long endless days in hospital, with Granny coming and crying over me, and me feeling hostile and confused, listening to pops all the time and the cricket scores on my headphones, trying not to think. And then Mum and me and Dan coming back to the flat and trying to get used to being without Dad. That was tough. Mum used to cry a lot at night, I could hear her through the wall, and Dan got sick of it all and joined the Army as soon as he was old enough. He'd got to get away, he told me. So there's just Mum and me, and she has to wear a special corset because of her back which she damaged, and we often have rows but they don't mean anything because we make allowances for each other. I don't go out much, and never to discos, though Pete keeps on to me to, because of my arm. Apart from the scar it got broken in two places and it's crooked, and it often throbs like mad. I wish they'd sawn it off and chucked it away, and I told Mum that once when she was going on about how lucky I was not to lose it.

Mum comes in with a cup of tea. She always gets up early, she doesn't sleep well.

"Come on, Chris, it's not a bad morning," she says.

I heave myself slowly up in bed. "Thanks, Mum."

"Don't be long," she says, like she always does. "Want an egg?"

I make yukky noises. Honestly, she knows I hate eggs! She says I'm too thin, but she's the one who's incredibly skinny. We usually have this same conversation, it's a morning ritual. She smiles and goes off, and I hear her switch on Radio 1 in the kitchen. I get up and wander about, wishing I didn't have to wear school uniform. I'd like Mrs Chadwick to see me in something more trendy, but what a hope! I pull on the boring old white shirt and grey trousers. I washed my hair the night before to make it look one degree better for today, but now I don't like it and I comb it back. It looks a mess and I wish I'd left it alone. I glower, and fiddle with it till Mum yells at me to get a move on.

I sit at the kitchen table nibbling a bit of toast, thinking about how pretty Mrs Chadwick is. She's tall and very slim, with blonde straight hair, and a sort of lively, interested expression. Her eyes are grey, with beautiful long black lashes. She's never sarcastic, even the girls like her, and everyone says she's not a big-head, and she's even knowledgeable about sport. She only came this term, when Mrs Carter left to have a baby. She always wears trouser-suits or beautifully pressed jeans and dark roll-neck sweaters—she always looks elegant, not tatty like most of the staff, as if they've stopped bothering.

"I don't believe you've heard a word I say," Mum sighs as I get up. And she's right, I haven't, only as a background hum to my thoughts. I give her a brief hug and she looks resigned but pleased. "I'll get the bread on the way home," I tell her as an olive-branch, and then I pick up my bag, and I'm on my way.

It's only ten minutes' walk to school, and I mooch along wondering where she lives. I've been trying to find out, but no luck so far. I wonder what her husband's like, and how old she is—pretty old, in her late twenties, I should guess. She never talks about herself, like some of the staff. I wish *I* was in the late twenties. I hate being fourteen, a stupid age, neither one thing nor the other. I don't like girls of my age, they make me feel awkward, and I've only got one or two friends like Pete. Most people think I'm weird because I'm too quiet. Pete tells me to come out and about with him, he's off somewhere most nights, but I take no notice. We haven't got all that in common, but I'm glad to have him to go around with at school. He's popular and good at most things. I'm not bad at English, it's my strong point, but I'm pretty hopeless at most other things, like maths. And sports aren't good like they used to be, because my arm lets me down, and I hate the look of it at P.E. I used to be good at swimming, but I never swim now, and they've given up trying to make me.

As I get near the school gates I think about giving myself a new image—how about dyeing my hair? I'm so ordinary I'm pretty nearly invisible. If I looked startling, maybe Mrs Chadwick would notice me more? Or maybe just blond streaks would liven up the general effect?

"Look out," says a familiar voice. "You sleep-walking or something?" I jump and go scarlet. Unbelievably it's Mrs Chadwick I've bumped into, too deep in my dreams to see her.

She's laughing and—bliss!—she walks along beside me. She's got a slow deliberate walk, I've noticed she never hurries. At first I can't say a word but after a minute my heart stops thumping deafeningly, and I try to think of something. She starts talking about an act from *The School for Scandal* she wants us to do for end of term. She's mad on drama, and so am I. She says she wants some of us to read for the parts today.

"You're going to have a go, Chris, aren't you?" she says.

I shake my head and mutter. "Oh, come on," she says coaxingly. "Of course you must. You've got a good speaking voice when you aren't nervous. Do me a good turn, have a try at least."

"I wouldn't be any good," I mumble. Two of my form cycle by, grinning derisively. Silly twits!

"How do you know? Ever done any acting?"

I make a big effort. "Yes, years ago when I was a kid, at my primary school," I tell her. "But—"

"There you are, then. I'll be disappointed if you don't," she says. "Well, see you later." And she smiles and goes off into the front entrance, where only the staff go, while I plod round to the cloakrooms at the back, thinking what an idiot she must think me, but immensely pleased because she wants me to try.

Pete's in the cloakroom, hanging up his anorak. All round there's such a noise we have to shout. I tell him about the play, and he says he wouldn't mind a part. He fancies himself a bit. I know he'd enjoy being up on stage with all the girls watching him. I say I might try.

"*You?*" Phil Carter says, grinning. He really is a big-head, and I can't stand him. He's always getting at me.

"Why not?" I say.

"Well," he says, "what about your arm?"

"What about it, what's that to do with it?" I snap.

"Yes, you shut up," Pete says.

Phil goes on grinning. "It'ud show up on stage," he says. "Even if you cover it up it looks funny."

I could kill him. He sees my face, and beats a hasty retreat. Suddenly I feel low. I realize it's daft of me to try. I go off to the formroom without listening to what Pete's trying to say. As I pass the mirror by the pegs I see my face, grim and stony, and I think what a drip I look. They say it's personality not looks that's important—well, my personality's lousy as well! I feel like crawling into a dustbin and clamping on the lid extra tight. Nobody would notice I wasn't around, except maybe Mum. It's not a consoling thought.

After registration we go to the lab for science. I work on an experiment with Janetta. She's O.K., quiet like me, and good at science. She takes charge and I just do as she tells me. We don't say much. At least she's not giggly like most

of the girls. Science leaves me cold. Mrs Bates walks
around criticizing. She got married last year, and sometimes she's O.K., but today she's right off. Must have had a
row with her husband . . . I think dreamily about being
married to Mrs Chadwick, and wake up with a jerk when
Mrs Bates approaches us. "Look out!" Janetta warns. She
looks at what we're doing, nods reluctantly, and moves on.
Janetta says: "That's a relief," but I pretend not to hear. I
feel tired, it's ridiculous, as if it's the end of the day instead
of near the beginning. I even wish it wasn't English next
period. That's really daft.

The bell goes and we clear up and depart. Janetta gets
overtaken by two other girls, and I walk on alone. I'm
wondering whether to do the audition or not, I can't decide.
She said she'd be disappointed if I didn't but that didn't
mean anything, I quite realize that. I dither. Will it make
things better or worse? My mind goes round in spirals. Phil
pushes past, and I think how I'd like to knock him over, but
he's a lot bigger than me, so I don't intend to try. I just
ignore him.

For English I find a seat cautiously near the back, and
decide I'll just play it along, see what happens. Maybe the
subject won't even come up, maybe she won't do the
readings today after all. I won't have to make up my mind
then. Pete comes and sits down beside me and says "All
right?" and I smile and say "Fine."

Then Mrs Chadwick comes in, carrying lots of copies of
The School for Scandal, and after chatting and a few jokes
she's handing them round, telling us not to be self-
conscious, just to try a part to help her out. Well, I can't
help falling for that. About half the form agree to try, the
other half, lazy lot, are happy to sit back and criticize.

She's picked a part with plenty of characters. They've all
got off-beat names like Sir Peter and Lady Teazle—those
are two of the main ones. She gets a handful of people to
try; they read through awkwardly, giggling a bit to start
with. It's a bit hard to follow, but you can gather it's meant
to be funny. She doesn't want anybody to *act* at present, she

says soothingly, just read the lines. Pete reads Sir Peter
Teazle, but he's not much good, poor old Pete. Then Phil
has a go, and goes over the top a bit, exaggerating,
overdoing it. He thinks he's been a hit, you can tell as he
looks round at the end. She nods, then looks enquiringly at
me. "You'll try Sir Peter now, Chris, will you?"

I swallow once or twice, but say "If you like", as if I
couldn't care less. People are staring. I notice Janetta
looking encouraging, and I suddenly think in a spurt of
defiance: "Well, why shouldn't I?" There's a rustle of
surprise, but Mrs Chadwick just nods and says good, and
gets some of the others to join in the scene.

Once we've started the reading it's not too agonizing. My
voice is croaky at first and my hands feel clammy gripping
the book, but I keep going, and when I look up once, while
one of the others is speaking, Mrs Chadwick gives me a
faint grin. I feel better, and to hell with Phil's truculent
stare.

"Not bad," she says at the end, rubbing her cheek
thoughtfully in a way she's got. "We'll have one more try
with the third group, O.K.? I can see there's plenty of
hidden talent among you, so nobody need be bashful!"

Everybody looks gratified, except the usual few awkward
customers who whisper to each other, trying to pull the
whole thing to pieces. There are just enough volunteers to
do it once more. To my surprise Janetta has a go as Lady
Teazle, and though you can tell she's nervous she's not
bad—she really flings herself into it, despite some of the
girls raising their eyebrows at each other. "That's the
stuff," Mrs Chadwick says at the end. "I reckon the whole
school's going to be pretty impressed with us, when we've
worked on this. Well, thank you all very much. You see
why I've chosen this act? It contains the nub of the plot, and
it's got some of the best comic scenes."

"Shall we do it in costume?" Janetta asks timidly.

"Oh yes, Mrs Wadley says she'll help. I know some of you
girls are good at making your own dresses, and there's no
reason why the boys shouldn't weigh in as well." I can see

Mrs Chadwick has given a lot of thought to this, and she
sounds really keen. She gets up and starts walking slowly
up and down. "It's set in the late eighteenth century, as I'm
sure you all know: the age of elegance, hoop skirts and
maybe powdered hair, though I doubt if we can run to
that." She drifts into detail, and I get edgy again. It
sounds much more of a production, much more elaborate
than I thought to start with.

We discuss it till the bell goes, and by the end she's got
most of us as keen to try it as she is. She's got this knack.
She tells us she'll put up the names of the people she's
chosen for the parts on the notice-board by 2 o'clock, and
that we'll make a start on rehearsals on Friday, and then
goes off in her leisurely way. Pete goes with her, having
volunteered to help carry the books—lucky Pete, he's
never backward in coming forward.

"Lots of fuss about nothing," somebody says. But
somebody else says "Oh shut up."

Of course I shan't be chosen, I think. It'd be ridiculous.
And if I *was*, I might mess it up. It's one thing reading a
few lines in class, that's bad enough, but to get on stage,
with all the school watching, ready to take the mickey . . .
Obviously it's not for me. Well, anyhow I read the part,
and so I didn't let her down, and I feel glad about that.

Pete comes back. "You weren't bad, Chris," he says,
trying not to sound surprised.

"Him?" Phil butts in, overhearing. "Who are you
kidding? It's bound to be me. Stage presence, that's what
I've got. Didn't you notice how they laughed at my lines?"

"No wonder," Pete says. "Can you blame them?"

Phil snorts indignantly. "Watch it," he warns.

"Chris was better than you by a mile," Pete goes on, to
my surprise.

Phil stares. "You're not serious," he says. "You don't
really think he'll get chosen, you're just being daft to
annoy me. Suit yourself."

He goes off. "What an idiot," Pete says. "Come on, I'm
starving."

I can't eat much dinner, my stomach's churning around. By 2 o'clock I'm at the notice-board. Mrs Chadwick always sticks to what she says, and I know the list will be there. There's quite a crowd milling around, and I can't get to the front at first. Then Janetta comes past me, trying not to look pleased. "I'm going to do Lady Teazle," she says, as if she's got to tell somebody.

"Great," I say, straining forward. Phil's black head is in front of me, and I still can't see. Though why I'm bothering . . .

"And Chris, you're Sir Peter," Janetta informs me.

"Me?" I gulp. I must look like a half-witted goldfish, opening and shutting my mouth.

Just at that moment Phil turns and comes shoving past. His eyes are blazing like headlights, he's so mad. He catches sight of me and shouts: "Oh, there you are—well, she's picked you. Big surprise, isn't it?"

"What d'you mean?" I say gruffly, wishing desperately I hadn't come, hadn't got into this at all. I hate scenes, and everybody's looking.

"Oh, come off it. You know why she's done it—she's so sorry for you, it stands out a mile," Phil says. "That's the only reason, it's obvious enough, isn't it?"

People just stand staring at us both. Pete says "Shut up—" but Phil doesn't take any notice. He goes on like a steamroller. "You'll ruin it for the rest of them, you realize that, don't you? You in costume with your stupid arm—how d'you think that'll look—plain ridiculous!"

For the second time that day I'd dearly like to kill him on the spot. I start to say something, but Pete's pulling me away. "Come on, Chris, don't waste time listening to him," he's saying urgently.

"Leave me alone, O.K.?" I say and go off, moving down the corridor with my head down, taking long shuddering breaths. He's right, that's the worst of it. I can't take any more. I can't do it, of course—I've got to find Mrs Chadwick and tell her, or write a note and put it in her pigeon-hole outside the staffroom. Somehow I've got to tell her right away. The bell's ringing for next period but I couldn't care less. Something feels like it's bursting in my chest. I'm aware of curious looks from everybody who sees me, but I don't care, I've just got to get away. It's now that I need that dustbin. I pull open the swing doors and burst out down the front steps, where strictly speaking we're not supposed to go, but what does it matter? And somebody's coming up and we collide.

"Not *again*," says an all too familiar voice. And would you believe it, I've cannoned into her for the second time in one day.

"I can't do it," I gasp, not looking at her. "Forget it, choose someone else, I'm sorry but I can't."

"Hey, Chris," she says, sounding concerned. "Come here." She leads me over to a bench under a may tree. Thank heaven no one's about here. "Sit down, calm down, and tell me what's going on."

I collapse on to this bench. "I suppose you're talking about the part in *The School for Scandal?*" she says. "What's all the excitement about? You read it well, and of course you'll be able to do it, why in heaven's name not?"

"No, I can't," I repeat. "Everyone will laugh, and I don't want them to, I don't want to spoil it."

"Why should they laugh?" she says with a steely note in her voice.

"Because of my arm," I mumble.

"Your *arm?*" she says, and she sounds genuinely at a loss. "What are you talking about? What's the matter with it?"

I look up, and I can see it's not an act, she really doesn't understand. She's never noticed—it's unbelievable. "It's scarred," I have to explain. "And it's not straight. I was in an accident years ago. So you see I couldn't possibly. Look." I hold out my arm so she can see.

"That's rubbish," she says, and she sounds grim. "That's no reason at all."

"It is, it is!" I burst out.

"That's a reason for trying harder, not giving up," she says shortly.

"You don't understand," I say mournfully. "You don't know how it feels."

There's a long pause. Then she says, "I understand all right. I'll tell you something. Years ago I came off my fiancé's motorbike on a corner. You didn't know I've got an artificial leg below one knee, did you?"

I can't believe it. I just gaze at her incredulously. She's so beautiful . . .

"So you see I understand all too well," she says. "But so what? We're all walking wounded if it comes to that. We've all got knocks and scars, whether people can see them or not, maybe inside us, maybe not. But that's no reason for giving up, is it?"

I feel deeply ashamed, stupid. "No," I say after a long long time, looking at the clusters of daisies in the grass near my feet.

"Well," she says, "what about it then? Are you really going to chuck it in?"

I think about Phil, but what he said isn't of much importance now. He doesn't know everything. Things are steadying down, and I can breathe more normally.

"I'm sorry," I say at last. "All right, I'll have a go."

"I should think so too," she says, and when I look across she smiles briefly. "Now for heaven's sake get back to your next class. You'd better apologize for being late, and say I kept you, O.K.?"

"Yes. All right," I say dazedly, and we both stand up.

"Another thing," she says. "Janetta will be scared stiff, so try and give her a hand, won't you?"

I nod. "See you Friday four sharp, for the first rehearsal," she says, and goes off up the steps into school. I watch her for a second. I know now why she never hurries. Then I go slowly round to the back of the building, back towards my classroom. It's strange, I feel about a hundred. But at the same time, funnily enough, I feel as if I'm just starting living all over again.

The Disappearing Abolisher

◇◇◇

Norman Hunter

Colonel Dedshott of the Catapult Cavaliers knocked heartily on the Professor's front door at exactly the same moment that Mrs Flittersnoop, the Professor's house-keeper, was knocking politely on his study door.

The Professor happened to look through the window and saw the Colonel on the step.

"Ah—er—um, my dear Dedshott, come in, come in," he said, making for the door.

Mrs Flittersnoop heard him say "come in," and she came in, tea tray and all, just as the Professor came out. The result was a most resounding teatime crash. Showers of brown bread and butter, hailstones of Bath buns, and plenty of steam.

Colonel Dedshott thought the Professor was having trouble with burglars or something and climbed hastily

through the window, where he got tangled up with the
Professor's latest invention, and had to be unravelled
like so much unsuccessful knitting.

"Well, Branestawm, what's the invention this time?"
said the Colonel, when they were settled with more tea,
fresh bread and butter, and the same Bath buns,
carefully dusted and re-arranged. "Talking pictures,
what? Or a new kind of machine for adding up one's
pocket-money, ha ha!"

The Professor looked at him through a special pair of
spectacles with little lids on them.

"An idea of far-reaching—er—importance, Dedshott,"
he said, reaching a bit far himself for another bun.
"Branestawm's Disappearing Abolisher."

"Wonderful," said the Colonel.

"If this lens," explained the Professor, pointing to a
sticking-out part of the machine, like a sort of sideways
chimney, "is directed towards any person or object within
a given distance and this red button is pressed, the said
object or person instantly—um, ah—disappears," finished
the Professor.

"But," he went on, "that is not all. You see these other
buttons, Dedshott, the white one is the reappearing
button. Press it and your disappeared object re—ah—
appears." He shut down the lids of his spectacles and
wheeled the invention forward. "The other button,
Dedshott," he said excitedly, "the black one, is the
abolishing button."

"Marvellous," said the Colonel. "Don't know how you
think of these things, by jove."

"There are two ways in which the object or—er—person
may be caused to vanish," continued the Professor. "They
may be simply—er—disappeared. That is to say, they
become invisible. They cannot be seen. But they are still
there, Dedshott."

"Ha, yes, of course," agreed the Colonel.

"The second method," went on the Professor, waving
spectacles and bread and butter about, "I call abolishing.

71

The Disappearing Abolisher

Having disappeared something or someone by pressing the red button, I have only to press the black button and they become abolished entirely. They are not only invisible, Dedshott. They are not there at all."

The Colonel said nothing. His head was going round and round, and he was content not to listen much, and agree with everything.

"When I have disappeared an object I can reappear it by pressing this white button," went on the Professor. "But the thing once abolished with the black button is gone for ever. I will show you."

The Professor focused his machine on the teapot and pressed the red button.

"Squee-e-e pop." There was a faint blue haze and the teapot vanished, but the tea made in it did not, which made a somewhat mess on the traycloth.

"I press the white button," said the Professor, "and, *voilà*." *Voilà* it was.

Back came the teapot with more blue haze and pops.

"Bravo! My word, Branestawm, jolly clever, what!" cried the Colonel.

"I have not—er—finished, Dedshott," said the Professor. He aimed his machine at a pink vase. Pressed the red button. Squee-e-e pop. Blue haze, no pink vase. Also not so many whiskers on the Colonel's moustache, as he had got himself a bit in the way of the disappearing demonstration.

"Bravo!" said the Colonel, who never cared much for pink vases, and didn't know about his whiskers.

"The vase has disappeared, but it is still there," said the Professor. "Just—er—pass your hands along the mantelpiece, Dedshott, and satisfy yourself on that point."

The Colonel felt about and found there was a hard, vase-shaped something where the pink ornament had been.

"I now press the black abolishing button," said the Professor.

He pressed it. There was a small bang and two puffs of smoke, one green and one dirty.

72

"Now see if you can find the vase," he chuckled.

The Colonel tried. There was no vase-shaped something.

"Completely abolished," said the Professor. "Nothing can bring that vase back again."

"Um—ha," grunted the Colonel.

"I am demonstrating the machine at Pagwell College next Tuesday," said the Professor. "Mr Stinckz-Bernagh, the science master, persuaded me to agree, but I—ah—fear I have very little experience of lecturing to boys. I wonder if you would—ah—um—care to come with me, Dedshott, by way of maintaining discipline."

Anything to do with discipline was the Colonel's middle name. Certainly he would be there. In full-dress uniform, wearing his medals and his best pair of spurs. The Professor could count on him. Discipline. If the demonstration depended on that it was an assured success, his word, by jove, yes, sir!

Getting the Professor's invention delivered to Pagwell College was a definitely touchy business. The manager of the Pagwell Furnishing Stores had kindly lent his biggest van and quantities of heavy gentlemen in aprons. The Professor insisted on riding inside the van with the invention to hold it together going round corners, as the van looked like being definitely shakable.

Once, when the van stopped suddenly at some traffic lights, the Professor sat on the machine and disappeared the van. He got it visible again only just in time to prevent three buses and a coal cart from running into it.

At Pagwell College most of the doors were too narrow to get the invention through. The moving-men, to whom the Professor had been doing a bit of complicated explaining on the way, were all for abolishing a bit of wall and unabolishing it after they had got the machine through, not seeing why an abolished thing had to stay abolished if a disappeared one could be visibled again.

At last the problem solved itself by two-thirds of the

invention coming off in the Professor's hands during the pushing about process. So it went in comfortably, and the Professor had it all fastened together again in the wrong classroom before anyone could stop him. This meant that the sixth form, all rather long-shaped boys in almost grown-up trousers, had to wedge themselves into little pale-blue desks in a room with joyous animals all over the walls. For the Professor had set his machine up in the Kindergarten.

Presently the door opened and in swept Mr Stinckz-Bernagh in a schoolmaster's gown, so flowing, and so much torn into strips at the edges, that he looked like a rapid black comet with too many tails.

"Good morning, Professor, we are honoured by your presence and looking forward to your demonstration which, I am sure, will be of the utmost educational value," he said in a very thin, crisp voice. Then he gathered up all the ends of his gown in both hands, dumped them on a table, leant on the top of them, and glared at the sixth-formers, who were sitting motionless, looking even more innocent and cherubic than the five-year-olds who usually sat in that room.

"Professor Branestawm has come here at great trouble and expense to lecture you on his own invention, which is exceedingly good of him. Three cheers for the Professor. Hurray! Hurray! Hurray!" said Mr Stinckz-Bernagh, who believed in doing all the polite things, but didn't believe in wasting any time in doing them. "May I remind you," he went on, "that there is a football match on Saturday afternoon in which I believe most of you hope to play. I trust it will not be necessary to postpone the match owing to some of you being kept in as a result of your not behaving properly during the Professor's lecture."

Then he gave out fifty lines all round to start with, and said that those who attended properly would not be expected to do them, swooshed his gown off the table, said, "Kindly begin, Professor," and disappeared out of the door in a shower of white chalk, dust, and black ribbons.

The Disappearing Abolisher

Professor Branestawm arranged his five pairs of spectacles in lecturing attitudes and began, while Colonel Dedshott stood by the door, military and menacing, ready to quell the slightest sign of revolt.

"Please, sir, may I go and get a handkerchief?" asked a boy with red hair and freckles, sticking up his hand.

"Er—um—ah, yes, of course," said the Professor, stopping in the middle of a complicated piece of explanatory finger-twiddling.

"Can I get one too, sir?" chirped a boy with a long nose that had ink smudges on it.

"I've left mine in my overcoat too," said another. "Me too," said several more.

The first ten minutes of the lecture passed to the tune of tramping feet as the class charged in and out for handkerchiefs. The Professor clashed his spectacles and felt as bewildered as his explanation of inventions usually made other people.

Colonel Dedshott, determined to have discipline at all costs, grunted "left, right, left, right, pick up your feet, now," as the scholars marched in and out on the handkerchief parade.

"Now this lens—" began the Professor again when everyone had all the handkerchiefs they could do with.

Red-head-and-freckles blew his nose like a trumpet.

"—when focused upon a given object," said the Professor.

Nose-blowing broke out in a chorus up and down the class.

"Please may I go and get a pencil?" asked Red-head.

"Yes, yes!" muttered the Professor. "Now this black button is most important, it is the abolishing—"

Crash! The Professor nearly jumped out of his spectacles. Had his machine accidentally abolished someone? No. Inky-nose had secretly tipped over the desk in front of him, boy and all.

By the time things had been put right way up and a second nose-blowing outbreak had passed, Colonel

Dedshott noticed that Red-head hadn't come back from getting a pencil.

"Ha, deserter, what!" he grunted. "Carry on, Branestawm, I'll fetch the defaulter. My word, yes," and out he strode, while the Professor turned his invention round and began on the other side.

Presently a desk lid was gingerly raised and some careful rummaging about began. Another desk lid went up, then another, and another.

"Have the goodness to shut those—er—desks and attend to my—ah—lecture," said the Professor, waving his near-sighted glasses threateningly.

Bang, bang, slam, crash! Desk lid-closing broke out like machine-gun fire.

Then the Professor began to notice something queer about the appearance of some of the scholars.

One was wearing a paper hat from one of the Kindergarten's drawing-books, so that it had some drawings of wobbly houses with wire smoke coming out of the chimneys chalked all over it.

"Stop that noise, by jove, what!" said the boy out of the side of his mouth in a Colonel Dedshott sort of voice.

Another pupil had made himself five enormous pairs of paper spectacles which he was wearing round his neck. Two others had their week's pocket-money fixed to their jackets with paper clips in imitation of Colonel Dedshott's medals.

The Professor made up his mind to take no notice of anything and get the lecture done as soon as possible. He charged on with complicated explanations, while the class gradually got more and more fantastic as paper hats and meant-to-be medals blossomed out in all directions.

"A peculiar mixture of light-rays is then directed upon the object," went on the Professor.

"Can I go out and wipe my boots?" said Inky-nose.

"The black button is vitally important." Three more paper hats and six rows of penny medals. "Please, sir, he's taken my nibs." "Here you see a lever which controls the focusing adjustment." Crash! "Give me back my pencil." "Please, sir, can I go out and bring myself back?" Thump! "Who put chalk in my ear?" "Press the white button."

In the midst of this educational uproar the door burst open and Colonel Dedshott returned trimphant, with Red-head grasped by one ear.

"By jove, what's this—mutiny!" said the Colonel. He advanced upon the class, every member of which was now completely equipped with paper hat, enormous spectacles, and pocket-money medals.

Then someone threw a ball of paper.

Pandemonium broke out.

The Colonel charged round knocking off paper hats with a ruler. Pocket-money clanged and tinkled over the floor. Red-head and Inky-nose barricaded themselves behind the blackboard and opened fire with bits of chalk.

Then the Professor lost his temper. He focused the disappearing abolisher on the rebels behind the blackboard and pressed the disappearing button. Bing! No Red-head. No Inky-nose.

But if the Professor thought that that was going to stop them he was mistaken. They had the advantage now. They were invisible, but still there. Unseen mischief occurred everywhere at once. Books flew through the air. Desks went crashing down. The Colonel's hat was snatched off and went dancing round the room, apparently on its own.

"Stop this at once, by jove, confound it, sir, what!" roared the Colonel. He and the Professor tried to chase the invisible ringleaders into a corner. They dodged easily. Then Red-head had an idea. Yes, he did. He ran invisibly to the disappearing abolisher. He focused it on the Professor. He pressed the red button. Bing! Then, "Oh help, no, no, don't do it, Red-head." He pressed the awful black button. Zim!

Professor Branestawm himself was disastrously disappeared and unreturnably abolished by his own invention!

The door flew open and Mr Stinckz-Bernagh shot in.

The entire class sat motionless and innocent-looking. Not a paper hat or a penny medal was to be seen. Angelic expressions were on every face, even on the faces of Redhead and Inky-nose, who were invisible, but probably didn't know it.

Colonel Dedshott blew up.

"Disgraceful sir, by jove, someone shall hear of this, what! Is this how you maintain discipline in your school, confound it, sir? Professor Branestawm comes here to give a lecture and your boys behave like rebels, sir. Yes, by jove, mutiny, nothing less!"

"Where is the Professor?" asked Mr Stinckz-Bernagh in a calm and meant-to-be soothing voice he used for pacifying fearsome parents who sometimes complained if their little boys got themselves whacked.

The Colonel looked wildly round. Suddenly it dawned on him what had happened. Almost. He guessed the boys had disappeared the Professor, but not that they had abolished him too. With a roar he swept Mr Stinckz-Bernagh into the waste-paper basket and slammed down the white button on the machine with such force that the two disappeared boys, Red-head and Inky-nose, literally sprang into view with a couple of bangs.

But, of course, no Professor Branestawm came back with them. He was abolished. Oh dear, oh dear, what would Mrs Flittersnoop do? How would Pagwell Council manage when they wanted queer machines for doing unnecessary things? Colonel Dedshott's head would never go round and round again, listening to the Professor's explanations. They would never have uncalled-for tea parties together, getting bits of the invention mixed up with the food.

Colonel Dedshott couldn't stand the thought of it. Why hadn't he smashed the invention as he had smashed so many others before it could do any real harm? Dashing an unmilitary tear from his eye, he snatched up the easel, swung it up and was just about to bring it down on the disappearing abolisher when a hand restrained him.

It was Mr Stinckz-Bernagh, with the waste-paper basket still clinging to bits of his gown.

"Wait a moment," he said. "There is, I think, a better way. The Professor explained the working of his machine to me. If it can abolish its inventor, it can be made to abolish itself."

He hurried out of the classroom and returned with a large mirror, which he set up opposite the machine.

"Ha!" grunted the Colonel.

"The light-rays focused on the mirror will be reflected back upon the machine," began Mr Stinckz-Bernagh, starting to talk like the Professor himself.

Colonel Dedshott didn't wait for explanations. Viciously he slammed down all three buttons at once.

Crash, bang, whizz-z-z; pouff, wallop, zang, bump!

Pagwell College shook to its foundations. The air was full of blue haze and pink dust. Colonel Dedshott and Mr Stinckz-Bernagh were flung simultaneously back into the waste-paper basket, which burst with another crash. The scholars tried to hide under the desks and got stuck there. Even the head master, who was at home with the tummy-ache, felt queer and shaky.

The disappearing abolisher had gone. Not so much as a lever or half a cog was left. The mirror was shattered to dust.

But, ah, oh, yes, but lovely and delightful and unexpected thing. In the place where the machine had been standing stood Professor Branestawm, clutching in one hand his five pairs of spectacles and in the other Mrs Flittersnoop's previously abolished pink vase.

"Er—um, dear me, most interesting and extraordinary," muttered the Professor.

Colonel Dedshott rushed at him with open arms and Mr Stinckz-Bernagh only just got out of the way in time to avoid being tangled up in a mixture of medals and spectacles.

The Disappearing Abolisher

It may be a scientific fact that when a Disappearing Abolisher is itself abolished its previously abolished victims become unabolished. But it is also possible that the Professor's invention, while appearing all too successful, had in reality some little but vital thing wrong with it which prevented really permanent abolishing. Still, the machine itself was abolished all right. Thank goodness perhaps. And for once the Professor had no need to think of new ways of using up an invention. Instead he set out to write a book on "What it feels like to be abolished," but found he couldn't remember.

The Sleepwalker

◇◇

Anthony Buckeridge

"Sir, please sir, were you alive in the olden days?"
Warburton asked. I don't think he was trying to be
funny: he was merely seeking information.

"It depends *how* olden," I replied. "I can remember a
time when twelve pennies made one shilling, and when
the radio was called the wireless, but I don't go as far
back as the Middle Ages, I'm afraid."

He considered this. Then: "What I meant, sir, was—
well, take something like sweets, for instance. Is it true
that before you grew old—or rather, when you were only
a boy—is it true that you could buy stuff like, say,
genuine mint humbugs for less than about ten pence a
quarter?"

I admitted it.

"Wow!" He looked at me with new interest. Clearly, I
was a relic of some bygone golden age.

"My grandmother's got a recipe for genuine old-fashioned mint humbugs," Warburton went on. "I've got some in my tuck-box. Shall I go and get you one, sir? Then you can see if they're the same sort you used to have when you were still only a youth, sir."

I saw now where the conversation was leading. "No thank you, Warburton," I said. "And, what's more, I'm not giving you permission to go down to your tuck-box after evening prep. It's time you were in your dormitory, and you know perfectly well that you're not allowed to take sweets up to bed with you." I pointed aloft and obediently he climbed the stairs.

I don't think he'd expected the ruse to work, but it had been worth trying. He made two more attempts to slip downstairs to the tuck-box room before lights out. First, he imagined an invisible blister on his heel which he thought might excite Matron's surgical curiosity: but as the dispensary was a mere ten-yard sprint from the tuck-box room I wouldn't let him go.

Then he wondered whether he might have left his missing garter on his football socks, and would it be a good idea to go downstairs and see? I said it wouldn't, and pointed out that if he persisted in undressing with his garter stretched over his scalp like a tight, elastic crown, he must expect it to shoot off into uncharted space.

As I put the dormitory light out I noticed a look in his eye which suggested that, so far as the harvesting of old-fashioned mint humbugs was concerned, Warburton still had another bolt to shoot.

I went downstairs and left the door of the staffroom ajar so that I could see the foot of the staircase. The Headmaster looked in shortly afterwards with a list of queries about why Ackroyd hadn't been doing his music practice, and whether we could change Form 4's geography period for an extra maths lesson on Thursday mornings.

I listened with half an ear. The other ear-and-a-half were listening for footsteps on the stairs; and ten minutes later they heard them.

I said: "Excuse me a moment, H.M." and walked out into the hall.

It's possible that if I had been alone, Warburton might have considered it a fair cop: but the Headmaster had followed me through the door, and his views on the subject of genuine, old-fashioned mint humbugs consumed under the bedclothes after lights out were known to be uncompromisingly stringent.

For a second Warburton hesitated and then, as it was clearly too late to retreat, he came on down the stairs towards us with his eyes shut and his arms stretched rigidly before him.

"Good heavens, the boy's walking in his sleep!" exclaimed the Headmaster.

I was tempted to point out that no fully-qualified somnambulist ever carries his arms at shoulder height or treads like a cat on spiked railings—except in fifth form productions of *Macbeth*. But I said nothing because I was thirsting with curiosity to know what the boy was going to do next.

He reached the bottom of the stairs and walked round us in a wide circle. It must have struck him that even the Headmaster's sympathetic concern would boggle at the idea of a sleepwalker tucking into genuine mint humbugs. So, with a masterly change of plan, he deliberately avoided the turning to the tuck-box room and glided along the corridor to his own classroom. He must have had some difficulty in restraining the impulse to look round and see if we were following.

The classroom was in darkness when we arrived. I switched on the light. Warburton was sitting at his desk with his history book open before him, studying a chapter on the Wars of the Roses through half-closed lids.

The Headmaster was impressed. "The boy's been over-working," he confided in a hushed whisper, and motioned me to tiptoe out of the classroom to discuss the next move.

"Let us consider," he went on when we were back in the

corridor. "Let us consider the best way of getting him back to bed while he is still asleep."

"I'm not so sure he *is* asleep," I said. "Why not just tell him to stop being stupid and get back upstairs at once!"

Politely, but firmly, the H.M. put me in my place. Would I kindly permit him to know the best way of dealing with a situation like this!

"On no account must we risk waking him: it's extremely dangerous," he told me. "At all costs we must avoid causing shock." He frowned in thought. "His mind is still on his work, you understand. It's not an uncommon situation: this sort of thing often happens with sensitive, highly-strung boys."

Sensitive! . . . Highly-strung! . . . *Warburton*! The boy was about as highly-strung as a shrimping net, but I let it pass. "Very well, H.M. What do you suggest?"

"Mm! I think I'll go and have a word with Matron before taking further action," he decided. "She's certain to know the best psychological approach. Just stay here and keep an eye on him for me, will you!"

When he had gone I went back into the classroom and sat at the master's desk. Warburton sat three rows in front of me, poring over his history book. As far as we two were concerned it might have been a normal evening prep.

I decided to call his bluff. "Come along now, Warburton. Stop playing the fool! I know perfectly well you're as wide awake as I am," I said.

He declined to fall into the trap, banking on the fact that I couldn't *possibly* know for sure. In silence the boy turned a page and went on with his reading.

What to do next? I couldn't let the silly little boy go on sitting there all night! But it seemed quite likely that this was what was going to happen unless . . . Unless I could give him the excuse he needed for going back to bed with no questions asked.

I looked at it from his point of view. He wanted us (the Headmaster and me, that is) he wanted us to believe that he imagined he was still in evening prep. All right, then, let's pretend he was! If I were to conjure up an imaginary preparation class and then tell them it was time for them to stop working and go up to bed, he'd be able to retire in good order.

I was rather proud of my little ruse. If the boy was awake (as I was pretty sure he was) he'd take the hint. If he really *was* asleep (as the H.M. seemed to think) he'd be bound to respond to a stimulus like that. Good psychological approach!

I rose from my chair and strolled slowly along the aisle between the desks—my usual practice when taking evening preparation.

"Keep the writing tidy, Ackroyd," I observed, affecting to inspect a non-existent exercise book in an empty desk in the back row. I moved a few paces towards the window. "Tt! Look at that smudge, Webster! Is that all you've done, boy! You've been wasting your time. You should be up to Exercise 4 by now!" My gaze swept along the rows of empty places. "Put your hand down, Matthews, you'll have to wait!"

I returned to the master's desk and looked at my watch. "Right! End of prep!" I announced loudly, as though addressing the class. "Books away, everybody, quietly . . . *Quietly*! Come along now, Warburton, put your work away!"

It was Warburton's cue and he took it. Closing his book, he replaced it in his desk and sat with arms folded, waiting to be dismissed.

It was then that I overplayed my hand. To be truthful, I'd rather enjoyed supervising a non-existent class, and I decided to put the finishing touch to the pantomine by dismissing the phantom form in the usual way.

"Stay in your places till the bell goes," I went on, "and then upstairs to your dormitories. No noise, mind, and no pushing on the stairs!" And I walked out into the corridor and rang the bell to signal the end of prep.

Warburton wasn't there when I looked into the classroom again a few moments later. Delighted with the success of my plan, I went back to the hall where I met the Headmaster and Matron hurrying down the stairs.

"Was that you ringing the bell?" the H.M. demanded.

"Yes," I said proudly. "All part of the psychological approach. End of prep, you see. A highly-strung boy with history prep on his mind was found to respond to a stimulus like that."

"Yes, but—"

"And it worked perfectly," I hurried on. "Warburton's gone back upstairs."

The Headmaster was furious. "Really, you might have had more sense," he fumed. "Don't you realize what you've done?"

As though in answer to the question a buzz of chattering voices and a patter of little feet sounded from the landing above. Ninety-seven pairs of little feet, in point of fact, pattering along the landing and down the stairs in their bedroom slippers.

Then I remembered! . . . That bell sounded all over the building, and when it was rung after lights out it was the signal for fire drill.

"Oh, my goodness," I stammered. "I'm most terribly sorry. I—forgot about fire practice."

"You forgot!" echoed the H.M.

"In the heat of the moment, you know. It was that boy, Warburton," I explained fatuously. "I was getting him back to bed."

"Instead of which you've got everybody else *out* of bed." There was no mistaking the terseness in the Headmaster's voice.

And no wonder! For by now the staircase was jammed from wall to banisters with a sleepy-eyed column of dressing-gowned figures yawning their way downstairs in response to the summons of the bell.

"Leave it to me! I'll stop them," I said, moving to the foot of the stairs. But the H.M. held up a restraining hand. "Too late for that now," he said.

He was right. Any attempt to reverse the stream in full flood would have led to chaos on the staircase. The confusion would have been indescribable.

"There's only one thing to be done," the Headmaster went on. "We shall have to *have* a fire practice and let them go through with the drill as though we'd organized it on purpose. Roll-call, inspection of premises—the lot!"

Scowling with disapproval he strode away to carry out the usual fire drill procedure in the assembly hall.

By now the head of the column had reached the foot of the stairs. Some still heavy-eyed with sleep, others wide awake and agog with excitement, they crossed the hall and disappeared down the corridor in the wake of the Headmaster. I assumed that Warburton was among them, but I didn't see him.

Ackroyd was the last one down the stairs. He arrived carrying Matron's cat which he had rescued from the Sewing room. Understandable, really. After all, he had no way of telling if it was a practice or whether the building was actually ablaze—and he was always a lad to be kind to animals.

I followed him to the assembly hall where the Head was waiting to check the attendance register. Ninety-six boys were present: one boy failed to answer when his name was called. The Headmaster scribbled a question mark against the absentee's name.

"Where's Warburton? Why isn't he here?" he demanded.

At that moment the door opened and Warburton hurried in. There was no trace now of his sleep-walking trance. Indeed, he looked particularly wide awake.

"Why are you late, Warburton? Where have you been?" asked the Headmaster.

The boy hesitated, and I wondered how he was going to cope with the question. My own guess was that, screened by the milling crowd in the corridors, he had slipped along to the tuck-box room for a handful of old-fashioned mint humbugs, now concealed in his dressing-gown pocket.

The Sleepwalker

The Headmaster was still waiting for an answer. "Come along now, Warburton, I asked you a question. Why didn't you come straight along to assembly with the rest of the school when the bell rang for fire drill?"

For a moment Warburton looked baffled. "Fire drill, sir?" he echoed blankly. And then a look of sudden comprehension passed over his features. His lips parted in a smile of understanding and his eyes opened wide. It was as though a light had been switched on in his brain.

"Oh, I *see*, sir," he exclaimed. "I see it all now. So that *was* the bell for fire drill after all!"

It was the Head's turn to look puzzled. "Naturally," he said. "What else would you assume it was for?"

"Well, I heard some of the chaps say something about it being the bell for fire practice, sir," Warburton explained. "Only I thought they must be making a mistake because—because—"

"Go on, Warburton. Because *why*?"

"Because Sir had just told us it was the bell for the end of prep, sir."

There was a suspicious bulge in Warburton's right cheek when I put the dormitory light out for the second time. In the circumstances I decided it would be best not to say anything more.

M13 on Form

◇◇◇

Gene Kemp

Told by X who never dares to give his/her name. The Cat's revenges are terrible and timeless.

"Books is comin'," yelled Mandy the Boot, blundering into the classroom in her father's size 12 army boots, and knocking Slasher Ormeroyd flying, which caused him to leap up with a mad roar and lurch to attack her, except that the Cat (Felix Delaney) paused in the middle of a poker game with Lia Tansy, Chinky Fred, and Tom Lightfinger to call out, "Cool it, Slasher," so that he hauled back his huge maulers for he always does what the Cat tells him. As we all do.

"What books?" enquired the Cat gently, for he was a great reader: crime and horror.

"A huge crate full. Old Perkins is turning 'em over an'

oinkin' like a ma pig with piglets. There's hundreds."

"Mr Pertins has comed back to us, doody, doody," crooned Daisy Chain, blue eyes beaming, bright hair bobbing. She loved Mr Perkins, and he was fond of her, not that he had much choice, M13 not being noted for its lovable characters. Mind you, we were all pleased to see him. He'd been absent on a course and the teacher they sent instead left in tears on Wednesday morning, making the rest of the week very tedious. The Headmaster took us. His name is Mr Bliss and it's a lie.

"That's great," said Bat Pearson, resident genius. "And about the books. We need new ones. Not that I read much fiction, haven't the time"—she was wading through *A Study of Bog Burial in Scandinavia and Europe* (funny place to bury people, said Mandy)—"but I like to keep Killer going and he can't stand *Little Women*."

Killer, six feet two and growing, nodded, for Bat does all his work. In return he's her Minder. Most of us need one. M13 aren't popular in the school, not that they're popular out of it either.

"I like Enid Blyton," cried Hot Chocolate, the class prefect. "I've read them all. Sir once said they'd made me what I am."

"Belt up," bellowed Hag Stevens from the doorway. "Mr Perkins is on his way." We were all so pleased to see him that we arranged ourselves nicely, looking keen and eager. And instead of sighing as he usually does at the sight of us, he smiled, which smoothed out all his wrinkles, like an American with a face lift.

"It's so nice to see you all again," he said warmly, and as if that wasn't enough he was dressed in cords and check shirt. Where was his old chalky? What was up? "As you know, I've been on a course, a language course, which I really enjoyed, and now I feel we can go forward with a new outlook."

"A wha . . .?" asked Brain Drain, dim even by M13's standards.

"A new outlook on the rest of our year together.

Speaking to you honestly, as your friend as well as teacher, that course came just in the nick of time, for I'd begun to despair at the thought of us struggling and drowning together . . . "

"I wunt let yer drown, Sir," interrupted Brain Drain, breathing hard, for uttering more than two words was always difficult. "I kin swim."

"Quite," Sir agreed. "Now let's see if my old friends are all here . . . Abdullah, Asra, Brian . . . "

Killer and Slasher were despatched to carry in the heavy crate, Bat, Lia and Mandy to organize the class resource centre. The rest of the school has a central area, but it was decided that M13 should just keep theirs in the classroom, after Tom Lightfinger flogged all the cassette players and musical instruments to some teenage pals to start a group.

"Any 'orror comics or girlie mags?" Slasher asked Killer hopefully.

"No, shurrup. The Cat looks after that side, and y'know he don't think it right for old Perkins to learn about such things. Not at his age."

Eventually all the splendid new books were arranged and the classroom transformed. Mr Perkins had done well, something for everyone: *Dr Seuss* for Brain Drain and Daisy and the Heap, *War and Peace* for Bat, *An Anthology of Horror* for the Cat. He beamed at us all.

"Yes, you shall soon get at them, but first something new for a new day. Has anyone a poem for me? A suitable poem, mind, Ormeroyd."

A mind-boggling hush fell for we always turned to the Cat or Bat or Mandy to represent us on these occasions and they all three despised poetry (wet, useless, boring). And then Brain Drain lumbered to his feet.

"I know one about an ickle worm." And he recited it while Sir grinned like a maniac.

"Jolly good," he cried. "They told me it would work. Good old M13. Don't let me down. Surely you must know a poem, Beatrice."

Bat stood up, grimacing horribly, embarrassed. "The only one I know is a dead boring one from Horace, about a smelly, skinny youth. Dates back to my classical hang-up last year. Sorry. Will that do?"

Sir nodded, and the Latin phrases hung in the classroom already quite well-known for its language. Killer smiled approvingly. His Bat was doing well even if no one could understand a word of it. And Tom Light-finger got up, brick red. "Know one about a dicky bird," he said, head down. "Learnt it in the Infants." One by one M13 made their offerings, the Cat last, with the lyrics of an obscure cult rock group.

A week later anyone walking into M13's classroom, and most people preferred not to, would have had to weave their way through poems everywhere—on the walls, on the windows, standing in displays, hanging on string, swinging in mobiles, for M13 had taken to poetry, writing poems, reading poems, reciting poems, illustrating poems. Mr Perkins had seen a miracle in his lifetime and walked on air. The school grapevine had it that the class had either gone barmy or had reformed at last. Actually, it was, as usual, the Cat.

Shoulders hunched, black glasses, white face, he said, "I want old Perkins happy. De poetry mikes him happy. So we get with de poetry. See?" We saw.

When it wasn't poetry, it was stories. M13 went book-mad, reading all of the time all over the place, even walking round the playground reading, with Killer and Slasher there to settle anyone foolish enough to find it funny. Those who understood what those squiggles on a page meant helped those who didn't.

So occupied were we, we didn't notice that the school's big issue was now Conservation. A famous celebrity had addressed the school on the subject and projects mushroomed everywhere. But it wasn't until a very pretty lady came to tell the school of the plight of a butterfly that was about to die out unless money could be raised to provide a Nature Reserve where it could breed that M13 realized it was needed.

"Dat poor ickle utterfly," muttered Brain Drain, moved.

Now despite everything: lies, thefts, vandalism, dishonesty, cheating, bullying, greed, truancy, you name it, M13's got it: despite all these or as well as, M13 has Heart. Disasters, we weep over disasters. Earthquakes bring contributions from us faster than anyone. Tom Lightfinger has been known to pinch the Save the Children pennies bottle from the corner shop to contribute to the class's gift. So when the very pretty lady said there was to be a prize for the best school contribution—a silver medal—and a framed poem about a butterfly written by the very pretty lady herself for the best class collection, there could be no doubt about it. M13 intended to get that prize, that poem on their wall.

No one needed to tell M13 about fund-raising. We have a natural talent for it: begging, gambling, sponsoring, busking, collecting, blackmailing, grovelling, stealing, shop-lifting, extorting, bullying, even selling, we went about it all in the way that suited each of us best. Yet in the final week but one, the grapevine informed the Cat that Hadley Grove School were the favourites, their rich parents being plushier than ours.

Mr Perkins was heard to remark with pleasure on the industry of his class, most pleased, most pleased. Reading, writing and money-raising thrived. An experienced teacher, though, every Friday he collected in the books that had worked the miracle (he thought) and checked them. That Friday only Bat's was missing and she promised faithfully etc. Mr Perkins went home. Happy.

On Monday morning all the shelves were empty. All the books had disappeared. So had every leaflet, magazine, poster and map in the resources area. His face sagged back into all those wrinkles, and he took the register, all present, except for Brain Drain.

"Right, what have you lot done with them?" He didn't look at all like that nice Mr Perkins. He looked more like Hanging Judge Jeffreys.

"Delaney, what have you organized?"

"Nothing, Sir." The Cat at a loss, for once. "Honest."

"You don't know what honesty is, Delaney."

But the Cat stood firm; it was nothing to do with him nor anyone else that he knew of.

"Then, Lightfinger, it just has to be you."

"No, no, no. I liked the books. They just took what I was half-way in the middle of and I haven't finished. And I dint read the ending first, for once."

"Hard luck," snapped Mr Perkins, cruelly.

And the door crashed open as the vast, shaggy head of Brain Drain appeared first, then the rest of him, waving a fistful of money.

"For de utterfly pome, Mr Perkins. For de pome. We win it now, won't we? Look at all de lolly. And I did it for you, Mr Perkins, becos you give me all dem pomes and I love pomes now."

"Brian, look at me and stop gabbling. Where did you get that money? And do you know what's happened to all our books?"

"I've conserved our books. Dey'll go on f'ever an' ever. An' dey gived me lolly for 'em. Look."

"But how?" groaned Mr Perkins.

Brain Drain was panting like an old train at full steam ahead. "Me auntie Mave. Cleanin' after school, an' she give me this dustbin bag an' I put 'em all in an' took 'em to our church for rebikin' . . . "

"For what?" Mr Perkins looked as if he was going demented.

"Recycling," translated Bat.

"An' they said what a good cause, and gived me money an' we'll win the pome now, wun't we?" he beamed. He sat down and then bobbed up again in the heavy silence. "Mr Perkins, Sir?"

"Yes, Brian?" came a low moan.

"I conserved them books and the utterfly, dint I?"

"Oh, Brian, you did, you did."

After a long time the Cat spoke, and for possibly the

first time in his life his voice was full of pity.

"M13. Listen. De kindness, get it? From now on we are going to be kind to Mr Perkins."

How M13 visited the recycling plant, rescued all the books (not very suitable anyway, they said), was spotted by the Mayor, also visiting, got its picture in all the papers (such keen children), won the school medal and the butterfly poem (more pictures in the papers—what fine, hardworking children, an example to others), so that at last Brain Drain could hang the pome on the wall—except they'd gone on to computer games by then—and as usual were hated bitterly by the rest of the school (good, hardworking, boring children) is another story.

The Fib

✧✧✧✧✧✧✧✧✧✧✧✧✧✧✧✧✧✧✧✧✧✧✧✧✧✧✧✧✧✧✧✧✧✧✧✧✧

George Layton

Ooh, I wasn't half snug and warm in bed. I could hear my mum calling me to get up, but it was ever so cold. Every time I breathed, I could see a puff of air. The window was covered with frost. I just couldn't get myself out of bed.

"Are you up? I've called you three times already."

"Yes, Mum, of course I am."

I knew it was a lie, but I just wanted to have a few more minutes in bed. It was so cosy.

"You'd better be, because I'm not telling you again."

That was another lie. She was always telling me again.

"Just you be quick, young man, and frame yourself, or you'll be late for school."

Ooh, school! If only I didn't have to go. Thank goodness we were breaking up soon for Christmas. I don't mind school, I quite like it sometimes. But today was Monday,

96

and Mondays was football, and I hate blooming football.
It wouldn't be so bad if I had proper kit, but I had to play
in these old-fashioned shorts and boots that my mum had
got from my Uncle Kevin. They were huge. Miles too big
for me. Gordon Barraclough's mum and dad had bought
him a Bobby Charlton strip and Bobby Charlton boots.
No wonder he's a better player than me. My mum said
she couldn't see what was wrong with my kit. She
couldn't understand that I felt silly, and all the other lads
laughed at me, even Tony, and he's my best friend. She
just said she wasn't going to waste good money on new
boots and shorts, when I had a perfectly good set already.

"But Mum, they all laugh at me, especially Gordon
Barraclough."

"Well, laugh back at them. You're big enough, aren't
you? Don't be such a jessie."

She just couldn't understand.

"You tell them your Uncle Kevin played in those boots
when he was a lad, and he scored thousands of goals."

Blimey, that shows you how old my kit is! My Uncle
Kevin's twenty-nine! I snuggled down the bed a bit more,
and pulled the pillow under the blankets with me.

"I'm coming upstairs and if I find you not up, there'll be
trouble. I'm not telling you again."

Oh heck! I forced myself out of bed on to the freezing
lino and got into my underpants. Ooh, they were cold!
Blooming daft this. Getting dressed, going to school, and
getting undressed again to play rotten football. I looked
out of the window and it didn't half look miserable. I *felt*
miserable. I *was* miserable. Another ninety minutes
standing between the posts, letting in goal after goal,
with Gordon Barraclough shouting at me:

"Why didn't you dive for it, you lazy beggar?"

Why didn't *he* dive for it? Why didn't *he* go in goal?
Why didn't he shut his rotten mouth? Oh no, *he* was
always centre forward wasn't he, because *he* was Bobby
Charlton.

As I stood looking out of the window, I started

wondering how I could get out of going to football . . . I know, I'd tell my mum I wasn't feeling well. I'd tell her I'd got a cold. No, a sore throat. No, she'd look. Swollen glands. Yes, that's what I'd tell her, swollen glands. No, she'd feel. What could I say was wrong with me? Earache, yes, earache, and I'd ask her to write me a note. I'd ask her after breakfast. Well, it was only a fib, wasn't it?

"You're very quiet. Didn't you enjoy your breakfast?"

"Err . . . well . . . I don't feel very well, Mum. I think I've got earache."

"You *think* you've got earache?"

"I mean I *have* got earache, definitely, in my ear."

"Which ear?"

"What?"

"You going deaf as well? I said, which ear?"

"Err . . . my right ear. Perhaps you'd better write me a note to get me off football . . . "

"No, love, it'll be good for you to go to football, get some fresh air. I'll write to Mr Melrose and ask him to let you go in goal, so you don't have to run around too much."

She'd write a note to *ask* if I could go in . . . ! Melrose didn't need a note for me to go in goal. I was *always* shoved in goal. Me and Norbert Lightowler were always in goal, because we were the worst players.

Norbert didn't care. He was never bothered when people shouted at him. He just told them to get lost. He never even changed for football. He just stuffed his trousers into his socks and said it was a track suit. He looked nearly as daft as me in my Uncle Kevin's old kit.

"Mum, don't bother writing me a note. I'll be all right."

"I'm only thinking of you. If you've got earache I don't want you to run around too much. I don't want you in bed for Christmas."

"I'll be OK."

Do you know, I don't think my mum believed I'd got earache. I know I was fibbing, but even if I had got earache, I don't think she'd have believed me. Mums are like that.

"Are you sure you're all right?"

"Yes, I'll be OK."

How could my mum know that when I was in goal I ran around twice as much, anyway? Every time the other team scored, I had to belt halfway across the playing field to fetch the ball back.

"Well, finish your Rice Krispies. Tony'll be here in a minute."

Tony called for me every morning. I was never ready. I was just finishing my toast when I heard my mum let him in. He came through to the kitchen.

"Aw, come on. You're never ready."

"I won't be a minute."

"We'll be late, we'll miss the football bus."

We didn't have any playing fields at our school, so we had a special bus to Bankfield Top, about two miles away.

"If we miss the bus, I'll do you."

"We won't miss the bus. Stop panicking . . . "

I wouldn't have minded missing it.

" . . . anyway we might not have football today. It's very frosty."

"Course we will. You aren't half soft, you."

It was all right for Tony, he wasn't bad at football. Nobody shouted at him.

"It's all right for you. Nobody shouts at you."

"Well, who shouts at you?"

"Gordon Barraclough."

"You don't want to take any notice. Now hurry up."

My mum came in with my kit.

"Yes, hurry up or you'll miss your bus for football."

"We won't miss our rotten bus for rotten football."

She gave me a clout on the back of my head. Tony laughed.

"And you can stop laughing, Tony Wainwright," and she gave him a clout, as well. "Now go on, both of you."

We ran to school and got there in plenty of time. I knew we would.

Everybody was getting on the bus. We didn't have to go to assembly when it was football. Gordon Barraclough was on the top deck with his head out of the window. He saw me coming.

"Hey, Gordon Banks . . . "

He always called me that, because he thinks Gordon Banks was the best goalie ever. He reckons he was called Gordon after Gordon Banks.

"Hey, Gordon Banks, how many goals are you going to let in today?"

Tony nudged me.

"Don't take any notice."

"Come on, Gordon Banks, how many goals am I going to get against you . . . ?"

Tony nudged me again.

"Ignore him."

" . . . or am I going to be lumbered with you on my side, eh?"

"He's only egging you on. Ignore him."

Yes, I'll ignore him. That's the best thing. I'll ignore him.

"If you're on my side, Gordon Banks, you'd better not let any goals in, or I'll do you."

Just ignore him, that's the best thing.

"Get lost, Barraclough, you rotten big-head."

I couldn't ignore him. Tony was shaking his head.

"I told you to ignore him."

"I couldn't."

Gordon still had his head out of the window.

"I'm coming down to get you."

And he would've done, too, if it hadn't been for Norbert. Just as Gordon was going back into the bus, Norbert wound the window up, so Gordon's head was stuck. It must've hurt him, well, it could have choked him.

"You're a maniac, Lightowler. You could have choked me."

Norbert just laughed, and Gordon thumped him, right

in the neck, and they started fighting. Tony and me ran up the stairs to watch. They were rolling in the aisle. Norbert got on top of Gordon and put his knees on his shoulders. Everybody was watching now, and shouting:

"Fight! Fight! Fight! Fight!"

The bell hadn't gone for assembly yet, and other lads from the playground came out to watch.

"Fight! Fight! Fight! Fight!"

Gordon pushed Norbert off him, and they rolled under a seat. Then they rolled out into the aisle again, only this time Gordon was on top. He thumped Norbert right in the middle of his chest. Hard. It hurt him, and Norbert got his mad up. I really wanted him to do Gordon.

"Go on, Norbert, do him."

Just then, somebody clouted me on the back of my head, right where my mum had hit me that morning. I turned round to belt whoever it was.

"Who do you think you're thumping . . . ? Oh, morning, Mr Melrose."

He pushed me away, and went over to where Norbert and Gordon were still fighting. He grabbed them both by their jackets, and pulled them apart. He used to be in the Commandos, did Mr Melrose.

"Animals! You're a pair of animals! What are you?"

Neither of them said anything. He was still holding them by their jackets. He shook them.

"What are you? Lightowler?"

"A pair of animals."

"Gordon?"

"A pair of animals, sir. It wasn't my fault, sir. He started it, sir. He wound up that window, sir, and I got my head stuck. He could have choked me, sir."

Ooh, he was a right tell-tale was Barraclough.

"Why was your head out of the window in the first place?"

"I was just telling someone to hurry up, sir."

He's a liar as well, but he knew he was all right with Melrose, because he's his favourite.

101

"And then Lightowler wound up the window, for no reason, sir. He could've choked me."

Melrose didn't say anything. He just looked at Norbert. Norbert looked back at him with a sort of smile on his face. I don't think he meant to be smiling. It was because he was nervous.

"I'm sick of you, Lightowler, do you know that? I'm sick and tired of you. You're nothing but a trouble-maker."

Norbert didn't say anything. His face just twitched a bit. It was dead quiet on the bus. The bell went for assembly and we could hear the other classes filing into school.

"A trouble-maker and a hooligan. You're a disgrace to the school, do you know that, Lightowler?"

"Yes, sir."

"I can't wait for the day you leave, Lightowler."

"Neither can I, sir."

Melrose's hand moved so fast that it made *everybody* jump, not just Norbert. It caught him right on the side of his face. His face started going red straight away. Poor old Norbert. I didn't half feel sorry for him. It wasn't fair. He was helping me.

"Sir, can I . . . ?"

"Shut up!"

Melrose didn't even turn round, and I didn't need telling twice. I shut up. Norbert's cheek was getting redder. He didn't rub it though, and it must've been stinging like anything. He's tough, is Norbert.

"You're a lout, Lightowler. What are you?"

"A lout, sir."

"You haven't even got the decency to wear a school blazer."

Norbert was wearing a grey jacket that was miles too big for him. He didn't have a school blazer.

"Aren't you proud of the school blazer?"

"I suppose so."

"Why don't you wear one, then?"

Norbert rubbed his cheek for the first time.

"I haven't got a school blazer, sir."

He looked as though he was going to cry.

"My mum can't afford one."

Nobody moved. Melrose stared at Norbert. It seemed ages before he spoke.

"Get out of my sight, Lightowler. Wait in the classroom until we come back from football. And get your hands out of your pockets. The rest of you sit down and be quiet."

Melrose went downstairs and told the driver to set off. Tony and me sat on the back seat. As we turned right into Horton Road, I could see Norbert climbing on the school wall, and walking along it like a tightrope walker. Melrose must've seen him as well. He really asks for trouble, does Norbert.

It's about a ten-minute bus ride to Bankfield Top. You go into town, through the City Centre and up Bankfield Road. When we went past the Town Hall, everybody leaned over to look at the Lord Mayor's Christmas tree.

"Back in your seats. You've all seen a Christmas tree before."

Honestly, Melrose was such a spoil-sport. Course we'd all seen a Christmas tree before, but not as big as that. It must have been about thirty feet tall. There were tons of lights on it as well, *and* there were lights and decorations all round the square and in the shops. Tony said they were being switched on at half-past four that afternoon. He'd read it in the paper. So had know-it-all Gordon Barraclough.

"Yeah, I read that, too. They're being switched on by a mystery celebrity." Ooh, a mystery celebrity. Who was it going to be?

"A mystery celebrity? Do you know who it is?"

Gordon looked at me as though I'd asked him what two and two came to.

"Course I don't know who it is. Nobody knows who it is, otherwise it wouldn't be a mystery, would it?"

He was right there.

"Well, somebody must know who it is, because somebody must've asked him in the first place, mustn't they?"

Gordon gave me another of his looks.

"The Lord Mayor knows. Of course he knows, but if *you* want to find out, you have to go and watch the lights being switched on, don't you?"

Tony said he fancied doing that. I did as well, as long as I wasn't too late home for my mum.

"Yeah, it'll be good, but I'll have to be home by half-past five, before my mum gets back from work."

When we got to Bankfield Top, Melrose told us we had three minutes to get changed. Everybody ran to the temporary changing room. It's always been called the "temporary changing room" ever since anyone can remember. We're supposed to be getting a proper place some time with hot and cold showers and things, but I don't reckon we ever will.

The temporary changing room's just a shed. It's got one shower that just runs cold water, but even that doesn't work properly. I started getting into my football togs. I tried to make the shorts as short as I could by turning the waistband over a few times, but they still came down to my knees. And the boots were great heavy things. Not like Gordon Barraclough's Bobby Charlton ones. I could've worn mine on either foot and it wouldn't have made any difference.

Gordon was changed first, and started jumping up and down and doing all sorts of exercises. He even had a Manchester United track suit top on.

"Come on, Gordon Banks, get out on to the park."

Get out on to the park! Just because his dad took him over to see Manchester United every other Saturday, he thought he knew it all.

The next hour and a half was the same as usual—rotten. Gordon and Curly Emmott picked sides—as usual. I went in goal—as usual. I nearly froze to death—as usual, and I let in fifteen goals—as usual. Most of the time all you could hear was Melrose shouting, "Well done, Gordon", "Get round him Gordon", "Good deception, Gordon", "Give it to Gordon", "Shoot, Gordon", "Hard luck, Gordon".

Ugh! Mind you, he did play well, did Gordon. He's the best player in our year. At least today I wasn't on his side so I didn't have him shouting at me all the time, just scoring against me! I thought Melrose was never going to blow the final whistle. When he did, we all trudged back to the temporary changing room. Even on the way back Gordon was jumping up and down and doing all sorts of funny exercises. He was only showing off to Melrose.

"That's it, Gordon, keep warm. Keep the muscles supple. Well played, lad! We'll see you get a trial for United yet."

Back in the changing room, Gordon started going on about my football kit. He egged everybody else on.

"Listen, Barraclough, this strip belonged to my uncle, and he scored thousands of goals."

Gordon just laughed.

"Your uncle? Your auntie more like. You look like a big girl."

"Listen, Barraclough, you don't know who my uncle is."

I was sick of Gordon Barraclough. I was sick of his bullying and his shouting, and his crawling round Melrose. And I was sick of him being a good footballer.

"My uncle is Bobby Charlton!"

That was the fib.

For a split second I think Gordon believed me, then he burst out laughing. So did everyone else. Even Tony laughed.

"Bobby Charlton—your uncle? You don't expect us to believe that, do you?"

"Believe what you like, it's the truth."

Of course they didn't believe me. That's why the fib became a lie.

"Cross my heart and hope to die."

I spat on my left hand. They all went quiet. Gordon put his face close to mine.

"You're a liar."

I was.

"I'm not. Cross my heart and hope to die."

I spat on my hand again. If I'd dropped dead on the spot, I wouldn't have been surprised. Thank goodness Melrose came in, and made us hurry on to the bus.

Gordon and me didn't talk to each other much for the rest of the day. All afternoon I could see him looking at me. He was so sure I was a liar, but he just couldn't be certain.

Why had I been so daft as to tell such a stupid lie? Well, it was only a fib really, and at least it shut Gordon Barraclough up for an afternoon.

After school, Tony and me went into town to watch the lights being switched on. Norbert tagged along as well. He'd forgotten all about his trouble with Melrose that morning. He's like that, Norbert. Me, I would've been upset for days.

There was a crowd at the bottom of the Town Hall steps, and we managed to get right to the front. Gordon was there already. Norbert was ready for another fight, but we stopped him. When the Lord Mayor came out we all clapped. He had his chain on, and he made a speech about the Christmas appeal.

Then it came to switching on the lights.

" . . . and as you know, ladies and gentlemen, boys and girls, we always try to get someone special to switch on our Chamber of Commerce Christmas lights, and this year is no exception. Let's give a warm welcome to Mr Bobby Charlton . . . "

I couldn't believe it. I nearly fainted. I couldn't move for a few minutes. Everybody was asking for his autograph. When it was Gordon's turn, I saw him pointing at me. I could feel myself going red. Then, I saw him waving me over. Not Gordon, Bobby Charlton!

I went. Tony and Norbert followed. Gordon was grinning at me.

"You've had it now. You're for it now. I told him you said he's your uncle."

I looked up at Bobby Charlton. He looked down at me. I could feel my face going even redder. Then suddenly, he winked at me and smiled.

"Hello, son. Aren't you going to say hello to your Uncle Bobby, then?"

I couldn't believe it. Neither could Tony or Norbert. Or Gordon.

"Er . . . hello . . . Uncle . . . er . . . Bobby."

He ruffled my hair.

"How's your mam?"

"All right."

He looked at Tony, Norbert and Gordon.

"Are these your mates?"

"These two are."

I pointed at Tony and Norbert.

"Well, why don't you bring them in for a cup of tea?"

I didn't understand.

"In where?"

"Into the Lord Mayor's Parlour. For tea. Don't you want to come?"

"Yeah, that'd be lovely . . . Uncle Bobby."

Uncle Bobby! I nearly believed it myself! And I'll never forget the look on Gordon Barraclough's face as Bobby Charlton led Tony, Norbert and me into the Town Hall.

It was ever so posh in the Lord Mayor's Parlour. We had sandwiches without crusts, malt loaf and butterfly cakes. It was smashing. So was Bobby Charlton. I just couldn't believe we were there. Suddenly, Tony kept trying to tell me something, but I didn't want to listen to him. I wanted to listen to Bobby.

"Shurrup, I'm trying to listen to my Uncle Bobby."

"But do you know what time it is? Six o'clock!"

"Six o'clock! Blimey! I've got to get going. My mum'll kill me."

I said goodbye to Bobby Charlton.

"Tarah, Uncle Bobby. I've got to go now. Thanks . . ."

He looked at me and smiled.

"Tarah, son. See you again some time."

The Fib

When we got outside, Tony and Norbert said it was the best tea they'd ever had.

I ran home as fast as I could. My mum was already in, of course. I was hoping she wouldn't be too worried. Still, I knew everything would be all right once I'd told her I was late because I'd been having tea in the Lord Mayor's Parlour with Bobby Charlton.

"Where've you been? It's gone quarter past six. I've been worried sick."

"It's all right, Mum. I've been having tea in the Lord Mayor's Parlour with Bobby Charlton . . . "

She gave me such a clout, I thought my head was going to fall off. My mum never believes me, even when I'm telling the truth!

A Very Positive Moment

<><><><><><><><><><><><><><><><><><><><><><><><><><><><>

Tim Kennemore

"I hate the first day of term," said Tamsin, stomping across the tarmac, hands stuffed crossly in coat pockets. She was in a bad mood, and prepared to hate almost anything. "Especially this term. I hate January."

"Everybody hates January," said Judith, who didn't see why Tamsin should have the sole rights to it.

"But *not as much as I do*," said Tamsin, in tones of dark triumph. "Christmas is all finished. Nothing nice happening for ever. It's all right for *you*. You've got your birthday in a few weeks. Mine's not till *August*." This reminded her of another grievance. "And I hate being the youngest in the form! I'm going to be twelve still, while everyone else is thirteen. I'll be the only one not to be a teenager."

"I don't think being a teenager is all it's cracked up to

be," said Judith, whose sixteen-year-old sister was currently verging on nervous collapse over her impending mock GCEs, and had boy-friend troubles to boot. Tamsin had been Judith's best friend since their junior school days; there were times when she wondered why, but on the whole Tamsin was worth it, even with her moods and moanings. Tamsin was smart, and always right in there at the thick of the action: action which would have left Judith-without-Tamsin hovering wistfully on the sidelines. "Anyway—who cares if you're the youngest? It doesn't show. It's much worse to be the smallest. Look at Gillian Phelps."

"I'd rather not," said Tamsin, and, rummaging in her satchel, she extracted that week's copy of The Magazine. The Magazine was Tamsin's Bible. It was cruelly named *Fifteen*, but it was amongst the second formers that it was most popular. It provided tantalizing glimpses of the sophisticated lifestyle that lay just around the corner. "Look at this dress, Jude. I mean, look at it. It's *beautiful*. When I'm a teenager that's what I'm going to look like. And I'm going to have matching leather boots and shoulder bag like these, and Mary Quant eye shadow and nail varnish . . ."

"Let me know what bank you're going to rob," said Judith. "Or are your parents going to start giving you a tenner a week when you turn thirteen, as a reward for having lived so long?"

Tamsin said nothing; there was nothing to say. It was the truth. On the allowance she got, she was often pushed, by Thursday, to find the cash for The Magazine, let alone the glorious things pictured inside it. By the week-end she was invariably stony broke, reduced to fingering the fabulous fashion clothes in Snazzy boutique, drooling with longing, while sales girls watched suspiciously. It was no good; she would have to find a way to make a lot of money. They'd be having Religious Instruction first lesson in the afternoon: she'd think about it then. Something like the principle of the Loaves and

the Fishes; little tenpenny pieces must be persuaded to
go forth and multiply into meaty ten pound notes. What
Tamsin could do with a tenner . . .

"Hey, you two—come here a minute." The little squirt
herself—Gillian Phelps, red-nosed and yellow-haired,
clutching a pad and a pen.

"The bell's going to go," said Tamsin, frostily.

"Not for another five minutes it isn't. Your watch must
be fast." Gillian Phelps was the kind of person whose
watch is always exactly right. "D'you want to bet ten
pence on who'll be elected form captain? Here's the odds,
look. Rachel Wilcox is favourite at three to one . . . but if
you fancy an outsider, what about Madeline Drury?
Fourteen to one—very generous odds. I must be mad.
One pound forty you'd get, cash, plus your original ten
pence back . . . "

It was no good. They had to look. Every time they
vowed *never again*, and every time they fell for it. Which
house would win the school sports? Whom would they get
for form teacher next year? Who would come top in the
science exam? Always they had a bet, and nearly always
they lost. The only winner was Gillian, crafty little
Gillian, the bookie's daughter. They knew this. The
whole form knew it. And yet . . .

"Tamsin Mitchell, six to one," read Tamsin, running a
finger down the list.

"You'd be favourite, except that you did it one term last
year."

"Hmmm. Rachel Wilcox, though? What've you made
her the favourite for?"

"Oh, everybody likes her. And she's never even been vice
captain. It seems like her turn. I've got a feeling about
Rachel this time."

"You're barmy. She's such a goody-goody little creep—
none of Sarah Pike's lot can stand her. Yeah—what about
Sarah Pike? She's much more likely. Go on then—*twenty*
pence on Sarah Pike. I'm confident."

"Twenty pence at seven to one," muttered Gillian,

filling out a slip. "What about you, Judith?"

"Oh, I'll put twenty pence on Sarah too," Judith said. It would be more fun if they were rooting for the same person. Judith herself was rated at fifteen to one; this, she thought glumly, pretty well summed her up.

Tamsin was still scanning the list. Right at the bottom, at twenty-five to one, was Caroline Stanmore. "You're wasting your time even writing her down." Caroline Stanmore was a nonentity, silent, spotty, sullen and stupid. When the class had to choose partners for gym, games or dancing, Caroline was always the one left out, the one who had to dance with the teacher. She never spoke in class; she had no friends. She didn't always smell very nice. "She's as much chance of being form captain as I've got of being Pope. She should be a million to one—and still nobody would bet on her."

"I'll give you fifty to one," said Gillian, hastily scribbling out the twenty-five. "There, look. Twenty pence gets you ten quid."

"No chance," said Tamsin, preparing to move on. It was a mug's game, this betting business. The only way to win a lot of money was to back somebody you knew couldn't win. So there was *no* way to win a lot of money. Still—Sarah Pike might come good. One pound forty was a whole lot better than a kick in the teeth.

The first day of term did have its good points. Assembly was more than usually prolonged and tedious —Tamsin tuned out when Miss Ramsay started ranting about "the thrills and challenges of the weeks that will unfold"—but after that there wasn't a thing to do until lunch-time, except to sit around gossiping in the class-room while the form teacher—a young, intense type called Miss Flynn—organized things like dinner arrangements, the exchanging of new books for old, and the election of form officials. And so slow, so earnest, so easily distracted was Miss Flynn, so subtly disruptive were Form H2, that it all took a very, very long time. Miss Flynn would make a move towards getting down to business, and Heather Gilmore or Sarah Pike would suddenly ask, what did you get for Christmas, Miss Flynn? Do you really believe in God, Miss Flynn? and Miss Flynn, who believed that her pupils were her equals, and that their every question deserved her serious attention, would answer, often at length.

Three people took no part in any of this. Caroline Stanmore, hunched at her desk, peering short-sightedly at a green exercise book. Gillian Phelps, in her corner, quietly counting money and jotting figures in her rough book. This was not unusual. The silence, however, of Tamsin Mitchell was altogether without precedent. She too, was scribbling figures in her rough book, an expression of furious concentration on her small round face. Occasionally, she looked up and gazed at the window, on to which small patters of rain had lately begun to dash.

"No," said Miss Flynn, "I'm not very well informed about the current pop charts, but I do think the Beatles wrote some very nice tunes." It was now ten-thirty: fifteen minutes before break. "Oh dear," said Miss Flynn. "We don't seem to have got very much done. I wonder if we've got time to vote for form captain . . . "

"Miss Flynn!"

"Yes, Tamsin?"

Tamsin had dropped her pen, and was now sitting bolt upright, paying full attention. "Miss Flynn—do you honestly think that form captains are a good thing? I mean, in a Comprehensive School where everybody's *equal*, do you think it's right to pick one person out, and say, sort of, O.K., you're more important than everyone else?"

Miss Flynn's eyes lit up. It was the sort of question, intelligent and concerning a matter of principle, that touched her soul. She had not been so moved since Madeline Drury had shyly asked her opinion on the topic of vivisection, later spoiling the effect by saying that *she* thought cutting rats up was more fun than almost anything.

"Well, Tamsin! Although there are sound arguments for that point of view, I must admit that I personally . . . "

She was off. "What are you doing?" hissed Judith to Tamsin. "What's all that you've been writing?"

"I've worked out a way to get some money. Just pray that it keeps raining. It's worth ten quid. *Each*."

"How? What d'you mean?"

And Tamsin leaned across and told her. "Now," she said, "this is what *you've* got to do."

" . . . therefore not incompatible with the principles of democracy," said Miss Flynn. The bell rang, abruptly cutting off the flow. "Oh dear—already? We really *must* get on with things after break, H2." She glanced at the window. "It'll be a wet break, obviously, so sit quietly in the classroom. The tuck shop isn't open till tomorrow. If you want to use the lavatories, please return here straight away. If you haven't got anything to do," she added hopefully, "you could get on with your reading of *A Midsummer Night's Dream*. We'd reached the beginning of Act Three . . . " The class shrank back as if in pain. Miss Flynn taught English. People like Miss Flynn always did. "Well, anyway, try not to make too much noise," she said, and scuttled off to the staffroom, where—they knew, because they'd seen through the door—she would instantly light one of the cigarettes she so eloquently pleaded with them never to touch.

Tamsin looked round surreptitiously. To her relief, most people seemed content to stay where they were, giggling and nattering in their little gangs. A few were making for the door, but they'd probably be back in time. Break lasted twenty-five minutes. "O.K.," she said to Judith. "Off you go, and for God's sake get it right."

Judith strolled out of the room, along the corridor, and down the steps towards the cloakrooms, keeping a sharp eye out for a suitable victim. Ah—there was just the thing, huddled against the wall, looking lost and terrified. A first former—one of those tiny grey undeveloped ones,

uniform spanking clean and immaculately pressed, hair
strained back in trembling ponytail. Judith advanced.
She was one of the tallest in H2, which was the reason
Tamsin had delegated this task to her. Height equalled
authority.

"Ah!" she said loudly. The first former looked up in
fright. Judith could see her little brain desperately
trying to work out what she had done wrong, and
wondering what was to be her punishment. "Would you
run along to room 14—you know where that is?"—
squeak of assent—"and tell Gillian Phelps and Caroline
Stanmore that Miss Ramsay wants to see them. They're
to wait outside her office until she fetches them in. Got
that?"

"Gillian Phelps and Caroline Stanmore," said the first
former, nodding furiously, and off she went, muttering the
names under her breath. Really, Judith thought, it was
marvellous being in the second year. It gave you
something to feel superior to. Mission accomplished, she
went off for a few minutes to loiter in the loo.

Tamsin, back in the classroom, was boiling herself up
into a fever of impatience. What was Judith doing? Had
she messed it up? Judith was normally reliable enough,
but . . . ah. Tap on the door, nervous little head peering
round, face like a peeled potato. What a little weed.
Where had Judith dug her up from? The weed was
looking alarmed; no nice safe teacher to whom she could
whisper her message. But "What d'you want?" called
Sarah Pike, and the weed unburdened itself, and fled.
Sarah relayed the message. Exit Gillian and Caroline,
Gillian shaking her head in bewilderment, no, she hadn't
a clue what it was about. She took her money with her,
Tamsin noticed, stuffed into her blazer pocket. Caroline
just trailed out, eyes obscured by greasy strands of fringe.
Caroline's eyes rarely saw daylight. Shortly afterwards,
Judith returned, strutting jauntily across the room with
the air of one who knows she has done well.

"Right," said Tamsin. She went over to Miss Flynn's

desk and banged the board duster on it. Clouds of chalk flew upwards; H2 looked up in surprise.

"Everybody listen," said Tamsin, "and listen carefully, because there's not much time. How would you all fancy making a tenner? A crisp ten pound note, one for each of you?"

H2 regarded her with deep suspicion. "Oh yeah?" somebody said. "You going into the betting business now, are you?"

"Sort of," said Tamsin. "I want to rig the election for form captain." Immediately there was a buzz of interest. "If we fix it so that we know who's going to win, and put a big last-minute bet on, we could get a whole load of money out of little Miss Millionaire Phelps." She had their full attention. Nearly everyone had had a bet with Gillian at one time or another; nearly everyone was poorer as a result.

"Who shall we vote for to be captain then?" asked Heather Gilmore, who had quite fancied her own chances, and was hoping it would be her.

"Caroline Stanmore," said Tamsin. Howls of indignation and scorn. That smelly slob? That revolting creature? She had to be joking. They'd never . . .

"Oh, don't be so stupid!" They really were morons. She's always suspected it. "What d'you want—to vote for Rachel or somebody? Rachel's three. We'd hardly make anything. It wouldn't be worth the trouble. Caroline Stanmore is *fifty to one*. Fifty. That means we'd win fifty times as much as we bet. I've worked it out." She picked up her rough book. "Twenty-seven of us in the class, minus Gillian and Caroline, makes twenty-five. If each of us contributes twenty pence, we could put a five pound bet on. And at fifty to one, that makes"—she paused for effect—"two hundred and fifty quid. Ten each."

There was a long, awed silence. A strange, yearning look was discernible in the eyes of form H2. Ten pounds. Mentally they were caressing the crisp brown piece of paper already. Skirts, shoes, visits to the cinema, the skating rink . . . money! Money could do almost anything, and none of them ever had enough of it. Ten pounds.

"It's a brilliant idea," said Sarah Pike, slowly. "But there's a couple of things bother me about it. Will she take a five pound bet? Nobody ever bets that much. She's bound to wonder."

"I don't think Gillian would wonder about anything once she actually saw the money. She'd be *begging* me to make a bet with it. She's not that bright. It's just a question of doing it really casually. Look, I don't know. I think she'll fall for it. If she doesn't, we haven't lost anything, have we?"

"No—but the other thing is, two hundred and fifty pounds is an awful lot of money. Even if she's got it, would she part with it? I mean . . . "

"She'd bloody well have to! A bet's a bet. If she didn't pay, nobody would ever bet with her again, and that would be the end of her little income. And of course she's got it! She's been bleeding all of us for a year—don't you think she's got all that cash salted away somewhere? Course she has. And you think we're the only ones? She does exactly the same with the kids in her street. And what about Junior School? Gillian Phelps has probably been taking bets since she learned to *write*. And if she hasn't got it, she can damn well get it off her father. Anyway—" she glanced nervously at the door, expecting at any minute that Gillian would walk back through it and spoil everything—"you've got to decide *now*. There's no time to argue. Yes or no?" Most people were nodding yes, and a few were already getting out their purses, but there were still some undecided and hesitant faces.

"Oh, come on," Sarah Pike said. "What're you all afraid of? That smarmy little snake has made enough money out of us in the past. It's about time she got taught a lesson. Who're the cowards who won't join in?" She glared balefully around the room. "Right. That's better. Now, if I start collecting the money . . . "

"Wait a sec," said Tamsin. Sarah's support had probably

clinched it, but she needn't start thinking she could take over, just the same. "First we've got to organize the election. We can't have everyone voting for Caroline, or nobody'll believe it. I mean, no one ever gets all the votes. This is how we do it. The two rows on the left—" she waved her arm—"you vote for Caroline. That's eleven votes. Then we've got to have another candidate with strong support, so that the next row must all vote for the same person—Sarah, say. So you six vote for Sarah, and I will too—that's seven. Everyone else vote for whoever you like, as long as it's not Sarah or Caroline. Just don't all go for the same person, that's all. Everyone got that?" They nodded as if hypnotized. With half of their minds they were in Snazzy boutique, browsing through blouses, trying on dresses. "Right. Money." Sarah got up and began collecting. "You do that side," Tamsin said to Judith, and she herself took the two rows in the middle.

"Ramsay never sent for those two at all, did she?" Sarah said to Tamsin as they passed in the aisle. "You fixed that." There was a mixture of admiration and envy in her voice. "You really planned it out."

"You have to plan things," said Tamsin, rattling silver, "Or they don't work. That reminds me." She raised her voice. "When Gillian comes back and I make the bet with her, *don't watch me*. Don't take any notice at all." She could just picture it: the whole form craning their necks and giggling, and Gillian cottoning on. They were so thick, H2, you practically had to tell them their own names.

By the time the money had been collected there were only three minutes left before the bell. Tamsin sent Judith to lurk outside the staffroom, waylay Miss Flynn when she emerged, lungs well coated with tar, and engage her in conversation.

"What'll I say?" asked Judith.

"You'll think of something," Tamsin said unkindly. She was rather worried by the amount of small change. There was one pound note, but all the rest was in silver:

five, ten and twenty pence pieces. "This won't do," she said. "We need a note. Who's got a five pound note?"

"Well—I've got one," Joanne Burke said, "but you can't have it, I need it. I mean, I'm going to Snazzy after school to get this blouse in the sale, and I can't carry all that silver . . . "

"Oh, shut up woffling and give us the fiver," said Tamsin. "If this comes off you can get three flippin' blouses." She tipped the money on to Joanne's desk; Joanne blinked, her eyes following the silver stream. It was like winning on a fruit machine. She hardly noticed as Tamsin extracted the five pound note from between her fingers. And just in time, for the door burst open and in came Gillian, snarling and raging.

"I'll get that bloody kid! Who was she?" She looked round the room, as if one of H2 might be harbouring the criminal inside her satchel. "Ramsay hadn't sent for us at all. I'm so mad I could kill someone. *Who was that kid who brought the message?*" There was a great deal of shrugging, and, to Tamsin's horror, some giggling. But then, somebody always was giggling about something: Gillian saw nothing odd in it, and went over to her desk, still cursing under her breath. Caroline Stanmore slipped inside the room like a shadow; the bell rang.

Tamsin sidled over to Gillian's desk. "Bloody little first form scum!" said Gillian by way of greeting.

"Throttling's too good for her," agreed Tamsin, perching nonchalantly on the edge of the desk. "Ah, well. How's the betting going?"

"Fine," said Gillian, instantly appeased. She brought out her list and pad. "Nearly everyone's had a go. There's been quite a bit put on Heather Gilmore. Hope she doesn't win."

"She won't," said Tamsin.

"You want another last-minute bet, then? It's your last chance."

"Maybe." Tamsin picked the list up again. "Caroline still at fifty to one, is she? Anybody backed her?"

"Nah. The wet weed. Stood by me outside Ramsay's office for fifteen minutes just now and didn't say a word. Wouldn't even have a bet! I think she's mentally ill."

"Oh. Not much point in putting money on her, then, I suppose. I'd be wasting my time."

"Oh, not necessarily!" Instantly, Gillian transformed herself to Salesperson. "All sorts of weird things happen, you know. I bet lots of people like her really. She never does any harm. And, I mean, even if they don't they might vote for her out of spite. I mean, nobody likes being form captain. It's a real drag."

You lying toad, thought Tamsin. She slipped her hand into her pocket and brought out the five pound note. "I was thinking maybe I'd have another bet. This is all I've got, though. I haven't got any change."

Gillian's eyes popped. She opened her mouth to say: "I can give you change", but thought better of it. "Sound little investment, a fiver," she said weakly. Her fingers were twitching. She had already mentally added five pounds to the not inconsiderable sum in her savings account.

"Yeah—but it's a lot of money. Too much to bet, really, isn't it? I found this fiver on the way to school, you know. I was walking along, and I looked down, and I thought, no, it *can't* be—and it was. So I was thinking just now, even if I bet and lose, I won't be any worse off than I was when I got up. And fifty to one is such a lot of money I could win . . . but, there, there wouldn't be much chance, with Caroline."

"I reckon you've got *every* chance," said Gillian, reaching for a pen and hovering over the betting slip pad. "Of course, it'll break me, if Caroline wins . . . "

"Better not do it, then . . . "

" . . . but I'll risk it," she said generously, tweaking the note out of Tamsin's hand with much-practised fingers. "Here's your slip."

"I'm sure I've just thrown five quid down the drain," said Tamsin sadly, heading back to her own desk, and winking gleefully for the benefit of anyone who could see.

Judith returned, with Miss Flynn two paces behind her, looking anxiously at her watch. "Really, H2, we have *no time to lose*. I hope you've been thinking deeply about the election for form captain—which of your fellow classmates has the necessary qualities of responsibility and leadership . . . "

"Oh yes, Miss Flynn," they chorused. Never before had they thought about an election quite so deeply. Judith scrambled to her seat and glanced enquiringly at Tamsin.

"We have lift off," said Tamsin, pointing to the betting slip which poked out of her front pocket. "All systems go. You did well, to keep her so long."

"I asked her to tell me some good books to read. She went sort of delirious. She said it was moments like this that made her certain she's found her vocation. What's a vocation?"

"I thought it was a holiday," said Tamsin, and shrugged; they'd always known Miss Flynn was mad, it was nothing new.

"Write down *one* name," Miss Flynn was saying, "and then fold up your papers. Think carefully. Don't automatically vote for your best friend. Look at her and *think*. Is she suitable? Is she worthy? If not, think again." This was too good to resist; in perfect unison the class turned, scanned their dearest chum thoughtfully, and shook their heads with mournful regret. "Everyone finished *already*?" said Miss Flynn. "Very well. Pass your papers forward." She collected the slips, took them to her desk and began to sort them, her mouth curving upwards into a knowing little smile. You could see her thinking: how meaningful this is. What a wonderful rehearsal for adult life. What a splendid introduction to the principles of democracy.

The class watched silently as Miss Flynn's busy fingers unfolded, smoothed, sorted. Little piles were beginning to form on her desk, and one pile was already visibly ahead of the field. Nothing can go wrong now, thought Tamsin, but her fingers, arms and legs were crossed just the same. She'd have crossed her eyes if she hadn't been watching the piles so closely. It was going to work. Ten quid—ten crisp tasty smackeroos. And suddenly it seemed rather unfair that she, the deviser and organizer of the whole scheme, she who had done all the work, should profit by not a penny more than everyone else. What had the rest of those subnormal nurds done except to reach into their purses? Tamsin was their agent, and agents were entitled to ten per cent of their clients' income. She'd have one pound from each of them—they could keep nine, and be grateful. Except for Judith, maybe, and Sarah, because they'd helped. That left twenty-two people—twenty-two pounds, plus her own ten, made thirty-two. Wow and double-wow. Thirty-two quids' worth of goodies. She could hardly imagine it. Never before had she had so much money to spend. And there were sales on everywhere! How could she possibly have hated January? It was a *brilliant* month.

"Well—we have a result," said Miss Flynn. Nobody breathed. This was the all-important moment. With a teacher less daft than Miss Flynn, the plan could never have worked. Anyone with half a grain of common sense would be aware of Caroline Stanmore's status, or lack of it, and would *know* it must be a fixed result. But Miss Flynn, as yet untempered by age and experience, was so idealistic, so full of belief in the good in everyone, so blind to harsh realities . . . wasn't she?

"In third place, with five votes," said Miss Flynn, "is Tamsin Mitchell. Second, with eight votes, and your vice captain for this term"—how she did love to build up the suspense—"Sarah Pike." Eight? It should have been seven. But then, Gillian and Caroline must have voted for somebody. "And the clear winner with eleven votes—your new form captain—Caroline Stanmore! A round of applause for Caroline, everyone." Tamsin turned to Judith in jubilation. *They'd done it!* The class erupted into a frenzy of clapping and cheers.

122

A Very Positive Moment

Miss Flynn beamed benevolently around the room.
Such nice, good girls! She herself had long been trying to
devise some method by which Caroline might be brought
out of herself a little. The poor girl was so very lacking in
confidence. And now this—this *remarkable* form had,
spontaneously, given her the boost she needed. Form
captain—it would be the making of Caroline. A very
special form, H2. So mature, so unselfish. And so clearly
delighted by the result. Except—and Miss Flynn's face
fell slightly—except for Gillian Phelps, who was really
looking most hostile. *Most* hostile. She looked, in fact,
almost murderous. Such a pity, one person showing
negative feelings at what was a very positive moment.
And now, here was Caroline rising to her feet and
making her way to the front of the room. Perhaps a short
speech of thanks and acceptance. Miss Flynn could
discern a change in the girl already. New spirit—new life
in those dull eyes. Caroline came up to her desk, bent
over and spoke.

"I'm not being form captain," she said. "It's some joke
they're playing. I won't do it. I'm not going to do it."

"Oh—but, Caroline! Of course, you don't have to if you
don't want to—but don't you think . . . "

"No," said Caroline. Miss Flynn stared sadly at the two
large red spots on her chin; so close were they that they
appeared to be on the verge of joining, blending into one
huge megaspot. Could spots do that? "I don't think," said
Caroline, "and I'm not doing it." Miss Flynn considered
launching into her "I shall feel that you're letting me
down personally" speech, but it was no use. Caroline was
already slinking back to her seat and to obscurity.
Sighing deeply, Miss Flynn rose to her feet, trying to
think of a way to tell H2 as tactfully as possible, and
without hurting any feelings, that their new form
captain would be Sarah Pike.

*

"Two hundred and fifty quid you owe me," said Tamsin.

"Get lost."

"I had a bet," said Tamsin, "on who would be elected form captain. Caroline Stanmore was elected. She got the most votes. Whether she accepted or not is nothing to do with it. Now, how do you want to pay?"

"Go stick your head in a micro-wave oven," said Gillian. "You cheating vermin. I don't owe you anything. The bet was on who'd be the new form captain. Sarah Pike's the new form captain. Nothing more to say."

Tamsin knew she'd lost. She knew where she'd gone wrong, too: she'd been too greedy. They should have voted for someone like Judith, at fifteen to one. It would have been so much simpler and safer—and though the rewards would not have been so great, Tamsin would still have been comfortably off with her ten per cent agent's fee. Still—she hadn't given up yet. "The bet was on who'd be *elected*," she repeated. "That's what you said."

"Prove it. And then prove you didn't cheat."

"Who's cheating? You shouldn't be so stupid as to take bets from people who decide the result of what they're betting on."

Gillian swung round in fury. "Look. Here's your rotten fiver back. Keep your lousy stake money. And that's all you're getting. As far as I'm concerned the bet never happened. I'm not standing here arguing with you all day."

"I beg your pardon," said Tamsin. "If you're not paying out on Caroline, you must be paying out on somebody else. Or have you decided not to have any winners this time?"

"I'm paying out on Sarah, of course," said Gillian, and then she remembered.

"Good," said Tamsin, "because I put twenty pence on her, at seven to one, and so did Judith. Here's the slips. That's two pounds eighty, plus our original forty pence, makes three pounds twenty, please." Just as well she'd had that bet on Sarah as insurance. At least she'd made *some* profit. It hadn't been a wasted exercise. One pound forty clear. And there were those gorgeous little pots of glitter nail varnish in the sale at Snazzy boutique . . .

The Mole

<><><><><><><><><><><><><><><><><><><><><><><><><><><><><><><><><>

Alison Prince

"Where is your tie, boy?" demanded Mr Lombard.

"In my father's car," said Guy. "Probably."

Mr Lombard placed the tips of thumb and third finger together like a chef analysing the precise flavour of his Béchamel sauce and asked, "What is this 'probably'?" He affected an extreme refinement of speech which would have seemed more natural in a small, neat man. Mr Lombard was neither.

Guy sighed. He never tried to be polite to Mr Lombard. It was a waste of time. "I spent the weekend with my father," he said. "It was his turn."

Mr Lombard refused to be embarrassed. "These domestic arrangements are of no concern," he said. "At school, you wear a tie."

"I don't," said Guy. "Not if it's in my father's car."

126

The Mole

There was a short silence while Mr Lombard stared at him menacingly. Then he said, "Wear it tomorrow."

"Probably," said Guy.

A general grin ran round the class as they attended half-heartedly to their English Comprehension. Guy's exchanges with Mr Lombard were always good for a laugh. Guy, sitting by the window, read the next question in his textbook. It said, "Why did Kenneth break the window in the back door?" Guy yawned. He wrote, "Because the stupid berk had forgotten his key," and stared out of the window. The sun shone dustily in the empty concrete yard. Nine tied-up black plastic bags of rubbish slumped against the wall of the Science block. They were the only non-geometrical objects to be seen. Otherwise everything was rectangular. Windows, doors, walls.

Above the straight line of the roof Guy could see the tops of distant trees. He gazed at them with a kind of hunger. There was another reality out there. The grass was so tall on the Common that he could only see the end of Nick's tail as the dog bustled about looking for moles. It was funny about the moles, the way they came to the top sometimes in this dry weather. Usually they were dead, but Guy had taken a live one away from Nick yesterday, squeezing the dog across the muzzle to make him drop it. The mole had broad pink paws coming straight out of its shoulders, and its fur was black and wet with Nick's saliva. When Guy had put it down among the tall grass it sank into the earth like a stone dropped into water. The grass had quaked a bit behind it and then it was gone.

"Guy Carter, get on with your work," said Mr Lombard.

Guy transferred his gaze from the yard to the teacher's face. He surveyed the blue chin and the full-lipped mouth and skirted round the eyes to linger on the greased-down black hair which was not allowed to wave as it should. It was merely corrugated. He was very ugly, Guy thought, as slick and black and fat as the plastic bags in the yard.

Because of the hot day, Mr Lombard had taken his jacket off and patches of sweat darkened his shirt under the arms. There was black hair on the back of his hands and more of it stuck out from under the pale blue cuffs. School was a pain, Guy thought. It was all so ugly that it actually hurt. There was no escape. Nowhere to sink away like a mole.

Guy's vacant scrutiny suddenly became too much for Mr Lombard's patience. "What is the matter with you, boy?" he roared, banging his fist on his desk. "Do you *like* being in detention?"

"No," said Guy mildly. He leaned over his textbook, hunching his shoulders as he read the next question. "What did Kenneth find in the kitchen?" For God's sake, Guy thought, anyone who's read the beastly passage knows he found a corpse in the kitchen. If they'd only give us the whole book we could find out how it got there instead of fiddling about with all this crud. "Body," he scrawled idly.

Mr Lombard had got up and was prowling along the rows of desks, peering over people's shoulders to see what they had written. Guy curled his arm round the top of his exercise book but Mr Lombard extended a hand to pick up Guy's wrist by the shirt cuff so that he could inspect the boy's work. Guy let his arm hang heavily from the pinch of cuff. He hated the man's smell.

"What is this, 'body'?" said Mr Lombard angrily. "You do not answer these questions with a single word, Carter, you write a proper sentence." His eyes moved up the page to the previous question. "'Stupid—berk'!" he read aloud in disbelief. The class shouted with laughter. "It's not funny!" he snapped, then returned his attention to Guy.

"So, Mr Carter, you think you are too clever to write proper English, do you?" He released Guy's cuff and Guy let his hand fall with a thump on the desk. He felt inert all over. Mr Lombard folded his arms. "And what is so special about you?" he demanded sarcastically. "Is there some exceptional quality which permits you to produce work of this disgusting nature and imagine that you can get away with it? Stand up, boy."

Guy heaved himself to his feet. There were a couple of covert cheers but most people were simply watching with interest. Mr Lombard stared at him. "No tie," he said. "And these trousers—what are they?"

Guy glanced down at his denim-clad legs and shrugged.

"I think these are jeans," said Mr Lombard, frowning at the indigo fabric. "Jeans are forbidden in this school."

There was a general groan. The jeans row had been going on for weeks. Guy could not resist a smile. "The dye's washing out," he said.

"What?"

"I dyed them," Guy explained patiently. "Last time you made a fuss I dyed them black. When I wore them to school the next day you said, 'These trousers are a great improvement'. But the dye's washing out so they're nearly blue again."

"Don't be stupid," said Mr Lombard amid giggles from the class. "You can't imagine I would believe such a story."

Guy shrugged again. "Believe what you like," he said.

Mr Lombard's eyes bulged in speechless fury. Then he said, "Detention. Four o'clock here, tomorrow afternoon."

Guy shook his head. "I'm doing one for Mr Williams," he said.

"Then you will write out a hundred times, 'I must not be impertinent'!" shouted Mr Lombard. "And do that work properly and give it to me first thing in the morning!"

"O.K.," said Guy. Seeking a last irritating shot, he added, "By the way—how do you spell impertinent?"

After break, it was Art.

"Beer-can denting," announced Miss Black. She took an empty can from the stack of them in the cardboard box beside her desk and held it up.

"Thought we was doing lino cuts," said Tony Baldwin,

indicating the squares of lino and tools laid out on each table.

"We are," agreed Miss Black. Her curly hair bobbed as she nodded at him encouragingly. "Just stick with it—all will become clear in a minute." Holding the empty can on the palm of her hand, she brought the edge of the other hand down in a vigorous Karate swipe which left the tin folded double. There was an ironic round of applause and she bowed. "Think nothing of it," she said.

"Can you tear up telephone directories?" asked Tony.

"No," said Miss Black, and gave him a look which said clearly that he had overstepped the mark.

"Oh, all right," grumbled Tony, subsiding. Guy grinned. He liked Miss Black. She was so skinny and fierce.

When the class was quiet Miss Black held up the dented beer-can and said, "This is the kind of thing you see everywhere. It's not an arty thing you'd only find in a school or a museum, it belongs out there in the real world." She nodded towards the expanse of windows. The Art room was so high up that there was nothing outside except sky, but Guy knew what she meant. "If you go into a fish and chip shop," she went on, "what do you actually *see*?"

"Fish and chips," said Gary Bates.

Miss Black pounced on this response gleefully. "I was *hoping* you'd say that!" she exclaimed. "It illustrates so beautifully exactly what I mean. People don't really see at all. They just think in labels. Fish and chip shop, bus, car, house. If you really *look*, even a pavement has a constantly changing pattern of tones and colours. Looking is wonderful. It makes life completely different."

Guy suddenly thought of the mole with its short, soft fur which moved either way so easily. It had a long snout and its paws were as muscular as a man's hands. He wished he could see it again.

"Now, really *look* at this can," Miss Black was saying. "Look at the way the letters go in and out with the dents. Look at the shapes in it."

The Mole

"There's lovely patterns of light and shade, Miss," put in Tracey Pammett, who fancied herself as being good at Art.

"Quite," said Miss Black rather drily. "But don't let yourself think in conventional artistic terms either, Tracey. Try and look at the thing as if you've never seen a can before. Never seen *anything* before."

"We don't have to do that to the cans, do we?" asked Susan Dogthorpe. "What you did?"

"Yes, everyone dent their own can," said Miss Black briskly. "If you think you're going to hurt your hand, bash the can against the side of the table, like this." She demonstrated, then added, "and if I see anyone bashing a table with a can rather than bashing a can with a table, there'll be trouble. Tony and Susan, give out the cans, please."

A bedlam of can-bashing broke out. After a few minutes Miss Black shouted, "Right!" and the class was gradually quiet.

"O.K., so that's your subject matter," said Miss Black. "You've changed a dull geometrical shape into an irregular, interesting one. Now I want you to look at it really carefully. Turn your can about and see which side of it looks most promising. Then make a drawing of it on the paper I've given you. Not a finicky drawing," she went on as some people groaned. "Just a drawing to fix in your mind what you've seen. That's why I've given you charcoal, so you can't get bogged down in detail. Then, when you've sorted out exactly what you want to do, you can work it out as a lino design."

"Yeah, but what's it for?" asked Tony.

"It's for *you*, you twit," said Miss Black with passion. "To help you open your eyes and get into really seeing things. It's a great and glorious fascination that will last all your life, and it's as good in itself as the sun shining."

"She's blooming nuts," Tony muttered to Gary, who sat beside him. Gary nodded.

"And we could always use our lino cuts for fabric

printing afterwards," said Tracey primly.

"Don't trump my aces," said Miss Black. "That was the surprise I had up my sleeve, dammit."

The door opened and the Headmaster came in beaming genially and followed by a gaggle of Japanese people who all seemed to be wearing black-rimmed glasses and dark suits. "So sorry to interrupt you, Miss Black," he said. "These visitors are from the Educational Arts Institute in Nagasaki and they're very keen to see the workings of an Art department in a British Comprehensive School. I wonder if you could give them a brief guided tour?"

Miss Black gave him a reproachful look. The Japanese bowed. The Headmaster cringed. "I've got rather a lot on this morning," he said in excuse as he retreated to the door. "Sorry I couldn't give you more notice—just a quick look round." With a last smile, he went out.

Looking at the class, Miss Black let her shoulders droop slightly and everyone giggled. Guy suspected that she had a reputation for a good Art department; they seemed to get a lot of visitors. It was becoming a bit of a bore.

"I'll be with you in a minute," Miss Black said to the Japanese, who smiled and bowed again. Several of them carried notebooks as well as cameras. She turned back to the class. "You know what to do," she said. "Start drawing what you find most interesting about the cans. I'll be back as soon as possible." She turned to the Japanese with a polite smile and said, "We'll start with the Pottery."

When the door was closed behind them a hum of conversation broke out. Miss Black never minded people talking in the Art room, so long as they were working.

Guy turned his dented can slowly round in his hands. It had contained fizzy orangeade and it was sticky. It reminded him of the plastic bags outside the Science block. Why did he keep thinking about those bags? They seemed to sum up all that was so dreadful about school. Nothing to look at except a row of plastic corpses.

Nothing growing. Nothing real. He hoped the dustmen would have collected the bags by lunchtime. He drew a half-hearted charcoal line on his paper. It looked wrong. He scrubbed at it with his sleeve and shifted the can round a bit. He wished Miss Black had thought of something else. He could see that she was trying to find something that would catch people like Tony and Gary on their own wavelength, but empty drinks cans were horrible. The part of the Common where the ice-cream vans stood was littered with them, and Nick had cut his paw on a broken bottle there once.

The class was getting noisier. Miss Black, Guy knew, would have explained exactly how to set about the drawing of the can before setting them to work; her abrupt disappearance had left everyone in a state of uncertainty. Cans were being thrown in the air and sometimes caught again and Gary, finding that his can still contained a trace of Coke, dribbled it on Tony's head.

"Geroff!" Tony bawled, pushing his friend in the chest.

"Go it, Tone!" someone else shouted.

"I can't stand Art," said Susan. "It's so mucky."

"What?" called her friend Jane from across the room, not hearing what Susan had said in the general noise.

"Can't stand blooming *Art*!" shouted Susan.

Tony was trying to stack several dented tins on top of each other, unsuccessfully. The noise was becoming deafening.

Suddenly Mr Lombard was at the door, glaring.

"And just what is this?" he demanded in the sudden quiet. He advanced into the room. "You think school is a place for hooliganism? Put those disgusting cans in the bin at once!"

"We can't, sir!"

"We're drawing them, sir!"

The virtuous explanations were almost as loud as the preceding rumpus. Mr Lombard stared round the littered room incredulously and Guy gave an inward groan. There was going to be a tedious outbreak of fuss. Why couldn't the beastly man mind his own business? Guy abandoned the effort to make a coherent drawing of the can and decided to go straight for the lino. The short, bulbous-handled knife had a vee-shaped blade in it. Guy picked it up and started to cut a line with it. A curl of line curved up from the blade's tip as he pushed it through the tough surface. He could hear Mr Lombard ranting on and tried to shut the voice away.

"You—Carter! What have I been saying?" demanded Mr Lombard. Guy did not look up. The cut had to curve to the left just before it reached the edge of the lino. The hair on the back of his neck pricked as he felt Lombard coming towards him.

"When I am speaking you will sit up and take notice, do you hear? You will *look* at me."

Guy glanced up. "Oh, all right," he said tiredly.

"I *beg* your pardon?" shouted Mr Lombard.

Guy was determined not to look at him again. He took a firm grip on the lino and drove the knife hard through it, sweeping round in a reckless curve. Abruptly, the knife broke out of its cut and ploughed into the forefinger of Guy's left hand, gouging through it from above the knuckle almost to the nail. Blood welled out—a lot of it.

"Shit," said Guy. He got up and rushed to the sink, where he turned on the cold tap and held his finger under it. He heard Tony say, "You better do some first aid, sir. The box is on the desk—Miss always gets it out ready when we do lino."

There was no answer. Guy pulled a mauve paper towel out of the holder and wrapped it round his finger. Blood seeped through it very quickly and dripped into the sink. His finger hurt a lot. Some cotton wool would be a good thing, he thought. He turned to see if Mr Lombard was doing something about first aid—and saw that the teacher was sitting down in the chair he himself had so hastily vacated. His head was bent and his hands hung slackly on his knees. His face was putty-white.

Guy advanced, nursing his finger in its paper towel.

The Mole

Blood dripped on the floor as he made his way across the room. He stood in front of Mr Lombard, staring at the black, corrugated hair on the back of the man's bent head. There were flecks of dandruff in it. "Mr Lombard," he said deliberately. Slowly, the teacher looked up. "What shall I do with this?" asked Guy, and took off the paper towel.

He had not expected the effect to be so drastic. Mr Lombard's eyes rolled upwards until only the yellowish whites were visible. His body slackened and he pitched sideways off the chair to crash down on to the floor, where he lay inert.

Susan screamed and Tony said, "Cor!" Everyone jumped up to stare at the fallen teacher and Guy retreated to the sink with his dripping finger. A surge of triumph made him feel breathless. He did not care if he bled to death. It would have been worth it.

Miss Black came in. "What on earth's going on ?" she asked. Mr Lombard was sitting up, groggily.

"It was the sight of the blood, Miss!" said Susan.

"Whose blood?" asked Miss Black.

"Mine," said Guy from the sink. Miss Black came across to look. She inspected Guy's finger calmly, then glanced up to say to the class, "Will you all please sit down. And I'd like no talking at all for a little while. Susan, bring me some cotton wool."

Mr Lombard had managed to sit on Guy's chair again. His face was ashen.

"It's not as bad as it looks," said Miss Black, mopping. "You'll live. I don't think it needs stitching but you'd better pop down to the Medical room and see Sister. Do you want someone to go with you?"

"No, thanks," said Guy. His eyes met Miss Black's for a moment and he noticed a flicker of amusement. He wondered what she really thought. Holding his cotton wool-swathed finger up like a beacon before him, he made his way out.

When he got back Mr Lombard had gone and the class

was working quietly. He had persuaded Sister that he needed his arm in a sling. May as well make the most of it. Miss Black looked at him and said, "O.K.?"

Guy nodded. Now that the excitement was over, despondency was beginning to settle again. His normal state at school was one of deep depression.

"You can't do lino-cutting one-handed," said Miss Black. "Would you like to draw something for the rest of this lesson, what's left of it?"

Guy thought. "I wouldn't mind doing a mole," he said. "If you had a picture of one I could copy. I sort of know what they're like, but it's difficult to remember exactly."

"I've got a stuffed one!" said Miss Black, pleased. "On loan from the Museum. There's an owl and a red squirrel and a weasel and a mole."

"I'll stick with the mole," said Guy.

The mole was in a glass case, among some rigid-looking grass. Guy didn't mind it being stuffed. Dead moles weren't any use to anyone. Nick wouldn't even eat them, although he'd gobble up a field mouse if he caught one. Guy began to draw, holding the paper still with the elbow of his left arm in its sling. He went on drawing when, at the end of the lesson, the rest of the class packed away their lino things. In a minute the bell would go and he would have to walk down the corridor with the others, past the pale blue doors with mesh-reinforced windows and the wire cages which nobody ever put their shoes in because they'd get pinched. And out into the concrete yard to talk and shout with the others and try to forget that he wanted to be somewhere else.

The bell went. "Off you go—quietly!" called Miss Black. With a few shouts of, "'Bye, Miss!" everyone bundled out.

Guy stood up.

"Are you in a rush for dinner?" asked Miss Black.

Guy shook his head. "You only have to stand in a queue for ages if you go early," he said.

She looked at him thoughtfully. Guy did not smile.

"Would you like to stay here for the dinner hour?" she asked. "You could finish that drawing. It's coming on well."

"Thanks," said Guy. Relief flooded over him. He sat down again and picked up his pencil. Miss Black watched him while he drew a blade of grass. Then she said, "Guy, *are* you all right?"

Suddenly Guy felt a terrible desire to cry. Out there, the feathery grass grew to his fingertips. Here, the pale blue doors, the bags of rubbish, the concrete, people like Lombard, were all part of an endless pain. He frowned fiercely at the mole's paws. They turned outwards from its shoulders for shovelling.

"I'll have to go," said Miss Black, leaving her question unanswered. "I'm on duty." She picked up her bag and went to the door, then turned. "It doesn't go on for ever," she said. "There's light at the end of the tunnel."

Guy nodded. "Yes," he said. "I suppose there is." He looked up. "Thanks for letting me stay," he added.

"It's O.K.," said Miss Black, and was gone.

The stuffed mole lay perfectly still. In the brilliant sunshine which poured in through the huge windows, its coat looked dusty. Guy pressed his nose against the glass case, staring at the painted background of meadow and sky. A small crack, he noticed, ran round the base of the mole's long snout, parting the dead fur to reveal white bone underneath. Guy sat back in his chair and let out his breath in a long sigh. At least, he thought, he was alive. He picked up his pencil again. Tomorrow he had better wear a tie.

Last Day

✧✧✧

Iris Murdoch

It was about three o'clock on a Friday afternoon when
Annette decided to leave school. An Italian lesson was in
progress. In an affected high-pitched voice the Italian tutor
was reading aloud from the twelfth canto of the *Inferno*.
She had just reached the passage about the Minotaur.
Annette disliked the *Inferno*. It seemed to her a cruel and
unpleasant book. She particularly disliked the passage
about the Minotaur. Why should the poor Minotaur be
suffering in hell? It was not the Minotaur's fault that it
had been born a monster. It was God's fault. The
Minotaur bounded to and fro in pain and frustration,
Dante was saying, like a bull that has received the death
blow. *Partite, bestia!* said the mincing voice of the Italian
tutor. She was an Englishwoman who had done a course
on Italian civilization in Florence when she was young.

138

Virgil was speaking contemptuously to the Minotaur. Annette decided to go. I am learning nothing here, she thought. From now on I shall educate myself. I shall enter the School of Life. She packed her books up neatly and rose. She crossed the room, bowing gravely to the Italian tutor, who had interrupted her reading and was looking at Annette with disapproval. Annette left the room, closing the door quietly behind her. When she found herself outside in the heavily carpeted corridor, she began to laugh. It was all so absurdly simple, she could not imagine why she had not thought of it long ago. She crossed the corridor with a skip and a jump, making a tasteful vase of flowers rock upon its pedestal, and went down the steps to the cloakroom three at a time.

The Ringenhall Ladies' College was an expensive finishing-school in Kensington which taught to young women of the débutante class such arts as were considered necessary for the catching of a husband in one, or at the most two, seasons. The far-sighted mammas of the social group from which Ringenhall recruited its pupils were not by any means as rich as they used to be, and they wanted quick results. Ringenhall was geared to the production of those results with the stringency of a military operation. Annette had been a pupil at Ringenhall for about six months. Her father, who was a diplomat, wanted her to "come out" in London, and had taken the view that a short period in an establishment of this kind would produce in his "cosmopolitan ragamuffin", as he called Annette, sufficient of the surface of a young English lady for him to be able to pass her off as such during the social season which he felt to be a necessary part of her upbringing, if not exactly its crown. Andrew Cockeyne, who had not lived in England himself since he was twenty-three, and indeed thoroughly disliked the place, which he found, though he would not have admitted it, both tedious and oppressive, had nevertheless taken care to send his son to his own public school. Annette's education, which was less important, and in the course of which she had learnt four languages and little else, had been picked up *un peu partout*; but it was essential in her father's view that it should reach its climax in no other place than London. Annette's mother, who was Swiss, had spread out her hands and assented to this arrangement, and if she had felt any scepticism about it she had kept it to herself.

Annette was nearly nineteen. Concerning Ringenhall she herself had not experienced a single moment of doubt. She had loathed it from the very first day. For her fellow-pupils she felt a mixture of pity and contempt, and for her teachers, who were called "tutors", contempt unmixed. For the headmistress, a Miss Walpole, she felt a pure and disinterested hatred. "Disinterested", because Miss Walpole had never behaved unpleasantly to Annette or indeed paid any attention to her whatsoever. Annette had never hated anyone in this way before and took pride in the emotion, which she felt to be a sign of maturity. Against the Ringenhall curriculum she had fought with unremitting obstinacy, determined not to let a single one of the ideas which it purveyed find even a temporary lodgement in her mind. When it was possible, she read a book or wrote letters in class. When this was not possible, she pursued some lively daydream, or else fell into a self-induced coma of stupidity. To do this she would let her jaw fall open and concentrate her attention upon some object in the near vicinity until her eyes glazed and there was not a thought in her head. After some time, however, she discontinued this practice, not because the tutors began to think that she was not right in the head—this merely amused her—but because she discovered that she was able by this means to make herself fall asleep, and this frightened her very much indeed.

Annette put her coat on and was ready to go. But now when she reached the door that led into the street she paused suddenly. She turned round and looked along the corridor. Everything seemed the same; the expensive flora, the watery reproductions of famous paintings, the much admired curve of the white staircase. Annette stared at it all. It looked to her the same, and yet different. It was as if she had walked through the looking-glass. She realized that she was free. As Annette pondered, almost with awe, upon the ease with which she had done it, she felt that Ringenhall had taught her its most important lesson. She began to walk back, peering through doorways and touching objects with her fingers. She half expected to find new rooms hidden behind familiar doors. She wandered into the library.

She entered quietly and found that as usual the room was empty. She stood there in the silence until it began to look to her like a library in a sacked city. No one owned these books now. No one would come here again; only after a while the wall would crumble down and the rain would come blowing in. It occurred to Annette that she might as well take away one or two books as souvenirs. Volumes were not arranged in any particular order, nor were they stamped or catalogued. She examined several shelves. The books were chaotic, but in mint condition, since reading was not a popular activity at Ringenhall. At length she selected a leather-bound copy of the *Collected Poems* of Browning, and left the room with the book under her arm. She was by now feeling so happy that she would have shouted for joy if it had not been for the delicious spell which she felt herself to be under and which still enjoined silence. She looked about her complacently. Ringenhall was at her mercy.

There were two things which Annette had wanted very much to do ever since she had arrived. One of these was to carve her name on a wooden bust by Grinling Gibbons which stood in the common-room. There was something solemn and florid about this work which made Annette itch for a blade. The wood was soft and inviting. However, she rejected this idea, not because the name of Grinling Gibbons carried, when it came to it, any magic for her but because she had mislaid her pocket-knife. The other thing which she had always wanted to do was to swing on the chandelier in the dining-room. She turned rapidly in the direction of that room and bounded in. Tables and chairs stood by, silent with disapproval. Annette looked up at the chandelier and her heart beat violently. The thing seemed enormously high up and far away. It hung from a stout chain; Annette had noticed this carefully when she had studied it in the past. She had also remarked a strong metal bar, right in the centre of it, on which she had always planned to put her hands. All about and above this bar were suspended tiny drops of crystal, each one glowing with a drop of pure light tinier still, as if a beautiful wave had been arrested in the act of breaking while the sun was shining upon it. Annette had felt sure that if she could swing upon the chandelier the music which was hidden in the crystals would break out into a great peal of bells. But now it seemed to be very hard to get at.

In her imagination Annette had always reached her objective by a flying leap from the High Table; but she could see now that this was not a very practical idea. Grimly she began to pull one of the tables into the centre of the room. On top of the table she placed one of the chairs. Then she began to climb up. By the time she was on the table she was already beginning to feel rather far away from the ground. Annette was afraid of heights. However, she mounted resolutely on to the chair. Here, by standing on tiptoe, she could get her hands over the metal bar. She paused breathlessly. Then with a quick movement she kicked the chair away and hung stiffly in mid-air. The chandelier felt firm, her grip was strong, there was no terrible rending sound as the chain parted company with the ceiling. After all, thought Annette, I don't weigh much.

She kept her feet neatly together and her toes pointed. Then with an oscillation from the hips she began to swing very gently to and fro. The chandelier began to ring, not with a deafening peal but with a very high and sweet tinkling sound; the sort of sound, after all, which you would expect a wave of the sea to make if it had been immobilized and turned into glass: a tiny internal rippling, a mixture of sound and light. Annette was completely enchanted by this noise and by the quiet rhythm of her own movements. She fell into a sort of trance, and as she swung dreamily to and fro she had a vision of remaining there for the rest of the afternoon until the boarders of Ringenhall, streaming in for their dinner, would make their way round on either side of her swinging feet and sit down, paying her no more attention than if she had been a piece of furniture.

At that moment the door opened and Miss Walpole came in. Annette, who was at the end of one of her swings, let go abruptly of the chandelier and, missing the table, fell to the floor with a crash at Miss Walpole's feet. Miss Walpole looked down at her with a slight frown. This lady was never sure which she disliked most, adolescent girls or small children; the latter made more noise, it was true, but they were often in the long run easier to handle.

"Get up, Miss Cockeyne," she said to Annette in her usual weary tone of voice. She always sighed when she spoke, as if wearied by her interlocutor; and as she never cared particularly about anything, so nothing much ever surprised her. This calm indifference had won her the reputation of being a good headmistress.

Annette got up, rubbing herself. It had been a painful fall. Then she turned and put the table straight, and picked up the chair, which was lying on its side. After that, she retrieved her coat and bag and the copy of Browning and faced Miss Walpole.

"What were you doing, Miss Cockeyne?" asked Miss Walpole, sighing.

"Swinging from the chandelier," said Annette. She was not afraid of her headmistress, whose claims to moral or intellectual excellence she had seen through some time ago.

"Why?" asked Miss Walpole.

Annette had no ready answer to this, and thought she might as well skip a point or two in the conversation by saying immediately, "I'm sorry." Then she said, "I've decided to leave Ringenhall."

"May I again ask why?" asked Miss Walpole.

She was an extremely tall woman, which was also perhaps one of the secrets of her success, and although Annette, too, was tall, she had to throw her head back if she wanted to look into Miss Walpole's eyes. Annette took a step or two away and receded until the line which joined her eyes to Miss Walpole's made a nearer approach to the horizontal. She wanted to look dignified. But as she moved away, Miss Walpole imperceptibly approached, gliding forward as if propelled from behind, so that Annette had once more to crane her neck.

"I have learnt all that I can learn here," said Annette. "From now on I shall educate myself. I shall go out into the School of Life."

"As to your having learnt all that you can learn here," said Miss Walpole, "that is clearly untrue. Your style of entertaining is distinctly Continental, and as I had occasion to remark the other day, you still go upstairs on all fours like a dog."

"I mean," said Annette, "that I've learnt all the things which I consider important."

"What makes you imagine," said Miss Walpole, "that anything of *importance* can be taught in a school?" She sighed again. "You realize, I suppose," she went on, "that your parents have paid in advance for tuition and meals up to the end of next term, and there can be no question of refunding that money?"

"It doesn't matter," said Annette.

"You are fortunate to be able to say so," said Miss Walpole. "As for the institution which you call the School of Life, I doubt, if I may venture a personal opinion, whether you are yet qualified to benefit from its curriculum. What, by the way is *that*?" She pointed to the Browning, which Annette was now slipping into her bag.

"That is a book which I wished to give to the library as a parting present," said Annette. She handed it to Miss Walpole, who took it with suspicion.

"It is a handsome copy," said Miss Walpole. "We are grateful to you."

"I should like a plate to be put in it," said Annette, "to say it is the gift of Annette Cockeyne. And now, good-bye, Miss Walpole."

"Good-bye, Miss Cockeyne," said Miss Walpole. "Remember that the secret of all learning is patience and that curiosity is not the same thing as a thirst for knowledge. Also remember that I am always here."

Annette, who had no intention of imprinting this disagreeable idea on her mind, said "Thank you," and backed away rapidly towards the door. In a moment she was hurrying down the corridor and jumping into the street.

The Fun They Had

<<<<<<<<<<<<<<<<<<<<<<<<<<<<<<<<<<<<<<<<<<<<<<<<<<>

Isaac Asimov

Margie even wrote about it that night in her diary. On the page headed May 17, 2157, she wrote, "Today Tommy found a real book!"

It was a very old book. Margie's grandfather once said that when he was a little boy *his* grandfather told him that there was a time when all stories were printed on paper.

They turned the pages, which were yellow and crinkly, and it was awfully funny to read words that stood still instead of moving the way they were supposed to—on a screen, you know. And then, when they turned back to the page before, it had the same words on it that it had had when they read it the first time.

"Gee," said Tommy, "what a waste. When you're through with the book, you just throw it away, I guess.

Our television screen must have had a million books on it and it's good for plenty more. I wouldn't throw *it* away."

"Same with mine," said Margie. She was eleven and hadn't seen as many telebooks as Tommy had. He was thirteen.

She said, "Where did you find it?"

"In my house." He pointed without looking, because he was busy reading. "In the attic."

"What's it about?"

"School."

Margie was scornful. "School? What's there to write about school? I hate school."

Margie always hated school, but now she hated it more than ever. The mechanical teacher had been giving her test after test in geography and she had been doing worse and worse until her mother had shaken her head sorrowfully and sent for the County Inspector.

He was a round little man with a red face and a whole box of tools with dials and wires. He smiled at Margie and gave her an apple, then took the teacher apart. Margie had hoped he wouldn't know how to put it together again, but he knew how all right, and, after an hour or so, there it was again, large and black and ugly, with a big screen on which all the lessons were shown and the questions were asked. That wasn't so bad. The part Margie hated most was the slot where she had to put homework and test papers. She always had to write them out in a punch code they made her learn when she was six years old, and the mechanical teacher calculated the mark in no time.

The Inspector had smiled after he was finished and patted Margie's head. He said to her mother, "It's not the little girl's fault, Mrs Jones. I think the geography sector was geared a little too quick. Those things happen sometimes. I've slowed it up to an average ten-year level. Actually, the over-all pattern of her progress is quite satisfactory." And he patted Margie's head again.

Margie was disappointed. She had been hoping they

would take the teacher away altogether. They had once taken Tommy's teacher away for nearly a month because the history sector had blanked out completely.

So she said to Tommy, "Why would anyone write about school?"

Tommy looked at her with very superior eyes. "Because it's not our kind of school, stupid. This is the old kind of school that they had hundreds and hundreds of years ago." He added loftily, pronouncing the word carefully, "*Centuries* ago."

Margie was hurt. "Well, I don't know the kind of school they had all that time ago." She read the book over his shoulder for a while, then said, "Anyway, they had a teacher."

"Sure they had a teacher, but it wasn't a *regular* teacher. It was a man."

"A man? How could a man be a teacher?"

"Well, he just told the boys and girls things and gave them homework and asked them questions."

"A man isn't smart enough."

"Sure he is. My father knows as much as my teacher."

"He can't. A man can't know as much as a teacher."

"He knows almost as much, I betcha."

Margie wasn't prepared to dispute that. She said, "I wouldn't want a strange man in my house to teach me."

Tommy screamed with laughter. "You don't know much, Margie. The teachers didn't live in the house. They had a special building and all the kids went there."

"And all the kids learned the same thing?"

"Sure, if they were the same age."

"But my mother says a teacher has to be adjusted to fit the mind of each boy and girl it teaches and that each kid has to be taught differently."

"Just the same they didn't do it that way then. If you don't like it, you don't have to read the book."

"I didn't say I didn't like it," Margie said quickly. She wanted to read about those funny schools.

They weren't even half-finished when Margie's mother

called, "Margie! School!"

Margie looked up. "Not yet, Mamma."

"Now!" said Mrs Jones. "And it's probably time for Tommy, too."

Margie said to Tommy, "Can I read the book some more with you after school?"

"Maybe," he said nonchalantly. He walked away whistling, the dusty old book tucked beneath his arm.

Margie went into the schoolroom. It was right next to her bedroom, and the mechanical teacher was on and waiting for her. It was always on at the same time every day except Saturday and Sunday, because her mother said little girls learned better if they learned at regular hours.

The screen was lit up, and it said: "Today's arithmetic lesson is on the addition of proper fractions. Please insert yesterday's homework in the proper slot."

Margie did so with a sigh. She was thinking about the old schools they had when her grandfather's grandfather was a little boy. All the kids from the whole neighbour-hood came, laughing and shouting in the schoolyard, sitting together in the schoolroom, going home together at the end of the day. They learned the same things, so they could help one another on the homework and talk about it.

And the teachers were people . . . .

The mechanical teacher was flashing on the screen: "When we add the fractions ½ and ¼—"

Margie was thinking about how the kids must have loved it in the old days. She was thinking about the fun they had.

Some other Puffins

HAUNTING TALES
Ed. Barbara Ireson

'Ghosts? No such things,' you may be thinking. But within these pages there are many different ghosts – exciting ones, eerie ones, romantic, sad and even funny ones – all so vividly real that they may make you change your mind so you become a ghost-fancier yourself.

THE SHEEP-PIG
Dick King-Smith

Fly, the sheep-dog, looked at her strange new foster-child with astonishment. The little piglet she called Babe had been won at a fair by Farmer Hogget and was surely destined to be fattened up for the family freezer – yet here he was wanting to herd sheep! So Fly taught him everything she knew, wondering what would happen when Farmer Hogget noticed what was going on . . .

THE GHOST OF THOMAS KEMPE
Penelope Lively

What kind of ghost was it that had come to plague the Harrison family in their lovely old cottage? Young James sets out to find the answer in this delightfully funny story, which won the Carnegie Medal.

THE CALENDAR QUIZ BOOK

Barbara Gilgallon/Sue Samuels

A lively and inventive quiz book which uses the months and special days of the year as a framework on which to hang a wide variety of questions – not just testing general knowledge but encouraging readers to find things out for themselves.

THE PUFFIN TRIVIA QUIZ GAME BOOK

Maureen and Alan Hiron and David Elias

A mind-boggling collection of Trivia questions, plus games for the younger members of the family. Carefully chosen and selected by three experts in this field, these questions are bound to baffle adult players but provide true equality for kids!

UP WITH SKOOL

A collection of children's own worst school jokes. Each section is introduced by a celebrity, including Sir Harry Secombe on Games, Roald Dahl on Punishment and Cyril Smith, MP, on the delights of school dinners.

SHADES OF DARK
Ed. Aidan Chambers

Eight original ghostly stories by distinguished and bestselling writers known for their ability to conjure up strange images and exciting stories.

DOLPHIN ISLAND
Arthur C. Clarke

Johnny Clifton had never been happy living with Aunt Martha and her family for the twelve years since his parents had died when he was four. So, when an intercontinental hovership breaks down outside his house, he stows away on it.

YOU REMEMBER ME!
Nicholas Fisk

Timothy Carpenter, a young trainee journalist, is sent to interview his idol, the dazzling Lisa Treadgold – and, like thousands of others, soon falls under her spell.

JEFFY, THE BURGLAR'S CAT

Ursula Moray Williams

Nobody who saw Miss Amity and her cat Jeffy walking to the shops each day would have believed that the old lady was a burglar. Only Jeffy knew the terrible truth and was determined to reform his wicked mistress. But all his efforts to prevent Miss Amity from backsliding were foiled when she took in a stray kitten, Little Lew, who turned out to be the perfect partner in crime . . .

DOG DAYS AND CAT NAPS

Gene Kemp

Ten stories about animals – and their human owners. Cats and dogs are particularly prominent, but mice, gerbils and other assorted animals also weave their way through this delightfully funny and off-beat collection.

THE BATTLE OF BUBBLE AND SQUEAK

Philippa Pearce

Sid and Peggy and Amy adore the two gerbils, Bubble and Squeak, but their mother detests them. A ding-dong family battle results, and it's very uncertain which side has the more ammunition. Another story by the author of *Tom's Midnight Garden*.

THE TURBULENT TERM OF
TYKE TILER

Gene Kemp

Tyke Tiler is very fond of jokes – that's why there are so many in this story. And Tyke is also fond of Danny Price, who is not too bright and depends a lot on his friend. In fact, medium-bright Tyke and medium-dim Danny add up to double trouble, especially during their last term at Cricklepit Combined School.

LIZZIE DRIPPING

Helen Cresswell

Everyone in Lizzie's village thinks she is a fanciful girl, so it's no wonder they won't believe her when she sees a witch. But Lizzie doesn't care because she knows that in all Little Hemlock there's no one half as interesting as this witch – anyway, it makes life far more exciting to have such an unusual friend.

LASSIE COME-HOME

Eric Knight

Lassie is sold to a wealthy family when hard times befall her owners. Taken hundreds of miles away, she does what many collies have done before her – she starts for home so that she can be faithful to a duty: that of meeting a boy by a schoolhouse gate.

PARIS, PEE WEE AND BIG DOG
Rosa Guy

An exciting and gently humorous story about three boys who hang around together on the streets of New York. They get into many scrapes, run into trouble with the police and try to avoid the bullying Marvin and his gang.

CHARLIE LEWIS PLAYS FOR TIME
Gene Kemp

Cricklepit Combined School, which produced Tyke Tiler and endured Gowie Corby, is now coping with five of the numerous Moffat family. Trish and the others find they have a new teacher for their last term at Cricklepit, a strict disciplinarian who believes in silence, segregation and sex discrimination. But for one member of the family the worst thing is that Mr Carter has a passion for music.

THE BOYS WHO DISAPPEARED
Margaret Potter

David's mother is admitted to hospital early for the birth of her twins, and his stepfather is called away to perform an operation on a politician in India. What is to happen to David? In this exciting story of quest and discovery, two boys learn how to shape their own lives.